ASHLEY TAYLOR

The Other Night

First edition

ISBN: 979-8-9855329-4-4

Proofreading by Esther W. Kiburi
Cover art by ACM/AAFT
Editing by Ashley Taylor

This book was professionally typeset on Reedsy.
Find out more at reedsy.com

To
Arnetter, Robert, Irma, Helen, and Arthur...

Thank You For Watching Over Me

"When the legend becomes fact, print the legend."

- CARLETON YOUNG AS MAXWELL SCOTT: "THE MAN WHO SHOT LIBERTY VALANCE"

Contents

Preface   iv

Acknowledgement   vi

I   Part One

Chapter 1   3
  Before A Fall   3
Chapter 2   9
  Friday Night in Outpatients   9
Chapter 3   29
  The First Stone   29
Chapter 4   34
  Mind Control   34
Chapter 5   39
  Three's Company   39
Chapter 6   43
  Kak Dela   43
Chapter 7   47
  All The Girls Standing in Line for the Bathroom   47
Chapter 8   53
  Rock and a Hard Place   53
Chapter 9   57
  Lost & Found   57
Chapter 10   61

Puzzle Box	61
Chapter 11	65
Friends Like These	65
Chapter 12	72
Lima	72
Chapter 13	75
King "Leer"	75
Chapter 14	93
You're Beautiful... Inside	93
Chapter 15	104
Crème de la Meow Meow	104
Chapter 16	113
A Party Ain't A Party	113
Chapter 17	119
Tall Drink of Water	119
Chapter 18	131
Bridget J—s, Baby!	131
Chapter 19	150
To Catch a Thief	150
Chapter 20	160
Buns of Steel	160
Chapter 21	169
The Importance of Being Frank	169
Chapter 22	181
Timeo Danaos et Dona Ferentes	181
Chapter 23	192
It's a Small World	192
Chapter 24	209
Daddy Lessons	209
Chapter 25	221
WITSEC	221

Chapter 26   230
   The Road Not Taken   230
Chapter 27   241
   Hard-ER   241
Chapter 28   251
   Yellow Brick Rainbow   251
Chapter 29   262
   Powder Puff Girl   262
Chapter 30   272
   Fringe Benefits   272
Afterword   279

About the Author   283

Preface

Content Warning: This book contains references to several forms of trauma/abuse/violence/suicide and may be mature for some audiences.

Reader discretion is advised.

If you, or anyone you know, has experienced trauma and are in need of support, know that you are not alone.

https://www.rainn.org/

https://988lifeline.org/

https://www.1800runaway.org/

https://www.stopbullying.gov/

https://www.thehotline.org/

https://www.thetrevorproject.org/

https://humantraffickinghotline.org/

https://www.hiv.gov/

https://naacp.org/

Acknowledgement

This book is a labor of love that would not have been possible without the support of my incredible family and friends. I want to thank God for never letting me quit, my beautiful parents, Michael and Robin, for fostering my love of writing and encouraging me to follow my dreams, my cats, Boomhauer and Pretty, for cuddling next to me while I wrote a story I am proud of, and my phenomenal friends: Cassandre, Tara, LaScharlene, Melissa, Angie, Shanelle, Esthervincia, Jennifer, Naya, Millie, Empress, and Jerrica. Their encouragement, care packages, and patience through the long nights, beta-reads, and torn-up versions of The Other Night have been a blessing.

I am humbled and grateful.

I

Part One

Chapter 1

Before A Fall

"**Alexa,** play Spotify!" Tori yelled. Her cats jumped in surprise as music blasted from the speakers behind their favorite perch.

Tori looked at the clothes strewn across her bed with a sigh. Her date for tonight had bailed. Oh well, at least she wasn't wasting an outfit.

"What a dick," she mumbled.

Her devoted but moody tabby, Shadow, swatted a paw at Tori as she walked past. The cats hated it when she started pacing, but that was how Tori did her best thinking.

"Knock it off," she muttered. Tori rubbed Shadow's chin absently. "At least he was hot." She shrugged. "Note to self—stop saying 'at least' to everything."

Hank, her oversized tuxedo, gave her the feline equivalent of an eye roll while he settled into a more comfortable position across her pillow. The cats had been Tori's closest companions since she was a teen and had seen their share of relationship disasters over the years.

Poor Shadow went into extreme hissing fits whenever Tori's most recent disappointment came over. In contrast, Hank maintained his dignity and never acknowledged the man's presence, past a dismissive flick of his tail.

Her latest dip into the dating scene was Gerard, a charming walking six-pack with a massive "Alpha-Male" complex. The macho shit was a turnoff, but his record-breaking post-sex recovery time was almost worth the (absolutely) problematic views he spouted on his alarmingly-popular podcast "Small Brainz." Some people don't deserve a platform.

Gerard the Sprinter (Tori wondered what his listeners would think of that particular honorific) had never passed a three-minute round in bed, but, given a chance to catch his breath, he was quick, hot, and ready to go again like 99-cent pizza.

"I knew better. Shit, I don't even like pizza!" she chastised herself.

Recognizing the warning signs of a lost cause hadn't taken long. Building codependent relationships with pathologically damaged men had given her an alarming amount of well-earned gray hair and forced Tori to unpack some unhealthy habits. Dating "potential" was no longer on her resume. Mostly.

"Here for a good time, not a long time," she mumbled, giving herself a mental pat on the back.

Gerard wasn't a significant loss. Their dates usually consisted of dirty looks thrown her way if Tori ordered more than a salad while she would mentally fast-forward to the part where her feet pointed to the ceiling. Everyone had baggage, but making herself miserable at dinner to appease a man would never happen again.

"Been there, done that, burned the t-shirt." she thought.

The side-eyes alone would have been a deal breaker, but she cut him some slack after learning about his weight struggles as a teen. Thinking of his now chiseled figure, Tori would have never guessed, further proof that looks can be deceiving. Still, that particular man-child was a great lesson in learning to "keep it casual," a foreign concept to the serial monogamist Tori was trying not to be. After living alone for a while, she relished not dealing with the stresses of a relationship. When Gerard first broached the subject, she was clear that she was in no rush to settle down, and happily, neither was he.
Tori hadn't been single for this long since high school. She wanted to enjoy her freedom and roll in her new bed alone—or as alone as you could be with two cats crowding you.

For three months, her sex life was semi-perfect until those wonderfully casual encounters ended dramatically, with Gerard declaring, "Tori, I want you to be my girl now." He traced his fingers across her stomach in a haze of post-coital bliss.

Gerard took Tori's panicked grimace as a yes, and she had been too shocked to correct him.

Six days later...

"That motherfucker!" Tori had successfully paced herself from mildly irritated to fuming. She grabbed her phone and typed a vicious text but hesitated to send it. She didn't want to be with him in the first place. Tori erased the message, throwing the phone on the bed.

"See...THIS is why I'd rather be single," she told Hank. A slight twitch of his whiskers made it clear he wasn't buying it.

Tori grimaced. "Note to self, stop talking to the cats...and to self." She needed to find something to do, or the rabbit hole of thoughts that Tori was running from might catch up and ruin her first work-free Saturday night in months. It was bad enough that she replayed incidents in her life whenever she slept, which barely happened anymore. PTSD was a bitch.

"Shit! I could've been working," Tori groaned when she glanced at the clock. It was too late to willingly log into her computer on the off-chance her boss was online. Tori shuddered at the thought.

"Fuck it!" Tori scrolled through her phone to see who might be available until a name made her smile. "Leslie's always down for a good time." Hanging out with her meant a night of soaking up obscene amounts of alcohol after the club with greasy plates of meat from a sketchy food truck.

In the morning, with bloodshot eyes and faint remnants of the previous evening's eyeliner smudged under their lids, they would feign enthusiasm at whatever fad workout studio struck Leslie's fancy that week. She chuckled, remembering the time they got banned from hot yoga. "Fuck splits!" They toasted afterward, laughing at their expulsion from one of the most peaceful forms of exercise. Workouts were always followed by brunch at Sugar's, a local hotspot with three hours of unlimited mimosas for twenty dollars.

During one of those outings, a chance encounter with a model scout who saw a budding Jennifer Anniston in Leslie's natural blonde hair and fair skin led to semi-steady work with an agency. Leslie had been hesitant initially, but it turned out to be an intelligent decision. After persuading her parents to let her try modeling in the city for a few months, Leslie's family name and densely stamped British passport made her a popular newcomer to New York's Instagram elite.

But the expiration date for their fun was around the corner. Leslie still needed to sign meaningful deals, and if she couldn't find a U.S. job willing to sponsor her visa, she would have to go home.

Worrying her lip, Tori texted, "Your favorite fuckboy bailed on me. Any chance you're free tonight?"

The phone rang immediately. "Are you OK? Wanna do cocktails and Thai?" Leslie asked, not waiting for a response. "I said I was going to meet up with a girl from the agency tonight, but I'd rather see you."

For some reason, Leslie's itinerary set her panic bells off. Did Tori have the energy for an all-night rager? Suddenly the thought of sitting home alone didn't sound so bad. "If you already have plans. We can totally go out another—" she tried.

"I haven't seen you in ages," Leslie scolded her. "We'll gauge how you're feeling, and if you're up to it, she can join us later. You have clothes here so don't bring anything with you. My place in an hour?"

Pride and the promise of fun won Tori's internal debate. *Never sit in the house and sulk.* She laughed. "Sure, I can do that." Thank God for friends who let you keep things you might need at their house, just in case.

"Perfect! Love you!" She hung up the phone before Tori could get another word in. Conversations with Leslie were like jumping double dutch: you needed to choose the perfect moment to hop in. Leslie would bulldoze anything in her path with youthful exuberance and a crisp English accent when her mind was made up.

Tori put the phone on the charger and quickly ran to the bathroom to shower. Thirty minutes later, she was out the door.

Chapter 2

Friday Night in Outpatients

Tori reread Gerard's message in the back of the Uber. *Fucking weirdo.* She should've joined the convent the day boys stopped having "the cooties." Life would have been so simple. Tori seriously considered it in high school until a fateful conversation with a nun ended that dream.

She hated the all-girl high school that her parents had forced her into. While it was advertised as an elite environment dedicated to "molding promising girls into distinguished young ladies," the reality was starkly different. The Rowan Academy for Young Women turned out to be a glorified finishing school still grappling with the stain of their segregated history, despite years of matriculating daughters of the area's most affluent residents of color.

Rowan girls did what they were told, like perfect little Stepford specimens. They even graduated wearing wedding dresses of pure white that had to be approved by their school's Mother Superior first.

They smiled on cue, spoke demurely, and held on tightly to their virginity until Mommy, Daddy, and Our Heavenly Father said it was alright on their wedding night.

Being a Rowan graduate meant something on paper, but the hefty price tag for attendance didn't buy much. The building was cold, the uniform was shapeless and an unflattering shade of burnt pea, the food was terrible, and Tori was getting bullied by a group of girls in her class. Too civilized for fighting, they turned to mean girl gossip, spreading vicious rumors about anyone who ticked them off.

"Pay them no mind. They're jealous," had been her mother's perfunctory response as she forcibly straightened Tori's posture.

"If only they knew," Tori had thought, promising to follow the advice anyway.

Her life was no picnic; by age 8, depression was a familiar friend.

The drama from her classmates was the icing on a shitty cake at the beginning. The first time she heard a rumor that she was a ho, she laughed it off. Impossible! Tori never went near a boy if she could help it. By the fiftieth time, Tori heard the rumor from someone who didn't even go to her school. The person that told her happened to know one of her bullies. It wasn't funny anymore. It's harder to kill rumors once they grow legs. They tend to follow you around like the permanent records teachers used to threaten children with.

One night, Tori fell asleep watching Sister Act 2 and woke up with a brilliant idea. Her teenage brain had worked out the perfect solution to ending the rumor mill: joining the convent. Being a nun would solve all her problems. No one would dare call a nun a ho…at least, not to her face. Plus, it was the perfect escape from a life of forced achievements. A nun didn't have to marry young, breed early, and die wearing pearls.

Realizing she needed practical advice, Tori turned to God—or the closest representative she could find: Sister Lenora, the school's religion teacher. She was a nun with a no-nonsense delivery and southern drawl, making her a trusted confidant amongst the girls.

At sixty-three, Sister Lenora was the youngest of all the nuns at the school. Her classes were meant to teach them how to serve the Lord (mainly by keeping their legs closed), but the lectures were often candid conversations about O (Oprah, not orgasms) and women's empowerment. With her top buttoned cardigan, penchant for picking up slang from students, oversized spectacles, and the subtle scent of talc wafting from her clothing, the girls thought of her as a sanctified Mrs. Doubtfire, minus the obvious. Add a rebellious streak for colorful handmade jewelry (that got her chastised by her Mother Superior) and a love of pop culture. It was heavily speculated that the Sister might've sown a few "wild" oats before taking the habit.

Excited, she had sat in that classroom and laid her plan out for the Sister.

When she had finished talking, Sister Lenora laughed so hard that tears rolled down her chin. "Tori, being a nun means no money, no honey, and a boss. This is…not the life for you."

She never opened up to Sister Lenora again. Disappointed, Tori had her first real kiss on her sixteenth birthday and never looked back.

Saved by the nun, go figure.

Almost 14 years had passed, and Tori still couldn't decide why the Sister chose those words. Was the Sister surprised at the question or shocked that the rumors weren't true? She remembered the way Sister Lenora's eyes had flickered across her body as she shot down Tori's idea. She wouldn't be surprised either way. Little Black girls are rarely considered innocent, and sporting 32-25-42 measurements as a preteen was akin to volunteering to wear a scarlet A in the view of the elderly white nuns. They never seemed to approve of how their deliberately frumpy uniform refused to hide her burgeoning body.

But Tori couldn't deny that the whole no money/no honey thing was pretty funny. It was an excellent time to revisit that idea. A peaceful life appealed to her now more than ever.

The Lord might forgive a few residual Gerard flashbacks, and she'd never have to pay high-ass rent in New York again.

This was not the life she had hoped for.

Adult Tori's funds consistently ran on dust bunny. She was almost two years into a messy divorce, and her boss was always one toe away from a well-deserved ass-whooping for treating Tori like shit. Every day was a test of her thinly drawn patience.

Divorce is weird. Tori hated the process almost as much as she loved being free of her ex. When he pretended to be civil, they drafted an agreement on who got what, who owed what, and how things would be split. Separating property was the least of their issues...until he realized Tori was serious about leaving.

Since then, her prayerfully soon-to-be ex-husband had done everything he could to prolong the process. Determined to drain her financially, the man demanded monthly bank statements to verify she wasn't earning an extra dollar without his knowledge. The whole thing was a mess, but she complied. Once he saw she wasn't fighting more, he had his lawyers ask the court to move their dates, often citing some new ridiculous items he wanted to add to the discovery list. Imagine hearing that court was canceled because your ex's lawyer wanted you to prove the date you bought the dual DVD version of Mean Girls and Clueless. He knew that was hers. Fucking ridiculous!

Tori needed therapy to unpack the trauma of that relationship when it was all over, but she couldn't afford it between lawyers and rent. Besides, her mother would probably have her involuntarily committed if she found out Tori paid a stranger to listen to her issues. That old-school logic was ass-backward. She chalked it up to collective generational trauma that black people weren't fans of therapy. Tori was already breaking the mold, as no one in her family had ever divorced. Staying married forever but living separately and dating other people was fine, but divorce...absolutely scandalous.

With no one to talk her through the emotional aspects, she tried what her friends called "broke bitch therapy," A.K.A. watching every Black rom-com she could find. After a while, Tori saw a pattern. According to every content Black woman in the movies, the way to happiness was through the Five Fs: Freedom, Faith, Fitness, Focus, and Fun. If you suffered enough and hit every milestone on the checklist, one day, a Shemar Moore look-alike would knock on the door, ready to fix your car and your heart. He could poke your cervix the right way, too, if you were fortunate.

Some of the F's on her list were easier than others.

Tori prayed twice a day, doused herself in essential oils and shea butter, tried to exercise 4 days a week, googled the seven stages of grief until she could recite them by heart, and subscribed to some YouTube astrologists for a lil' razzle-dazzle (Tori kept that one a secret—her mother would've called an exorcist.) She had a few false starts, but for the first time in a long time, Tori felt hope.

Those broken-hearted workouts helped the depression weight she had gained during the lowest points of their relationship fly off while Tori threw herself into her work. Having a focus that he couldn't taint kept her mind occupied. As for fun, she started small—sneaking wine and charcuterie boards into the theater to watch matinees. Tori was content with those outings for a while, using them to help her tiptoe further into the world until a solo visit to the zoo put the kibosh on that. A woman had walked past her wearing a cat-shaped hat, bedazzled cat sweater, and a purse with whiskers glued on and winked at Tori as she bought her ticket.

Being a cat lady wasn't the worst option, but the woman looked at Tori like she saw a kindred spirit.

Ah, fuck. Can a nun curse you? She had wondered, watching the woman walk away.

Deciding to take a hard pass on her preordained spinsterhood, Tori turned to her pushy but well-meaning friends. Their advice; the quickest way to get over her heartbreak was by getting under someone else.

"Add a sixth F to your list!" They cackled.

It had taken a year to build up the courage for that.

The driver hit a speed bump, bringing Tori out of her reverie. On the radio, a song her Grandma used to play crooned, "...who gives a damn if you're a Capricorn or a Ram." She smiled, willing herself to think of happier times. Drawing a blank, she sighed. *It was worth a shot.*

A failed marriage under her belt before she turned 30. What a cliche. No one could say she hadn't tried to work things out first. She had sat down with her ex more than once, desperate to figure out how to save their marriage. He promised to get help. She promised to let go of the past. They both lied. He went to one A.A. meeting, stole their bible, and refused to complete couples therapy.

"We don't need outsiders in our business," he declared. "Just stop being a fucking nag."

Tori bit her tongue, letting it go until he threw her into the wall at a family party. The scuffle that followed involved blows thrown between them in the middle of the street.

"Don't leave me. You can't..." he had cried a few hours later, drunkenly smearing vomit across the floor as he crawled to her. In an out-of-body experience, she numbly watched him as he pulled at her clothes with foul-sticky hands pleading for another chance.

Tori spoke to him gently, taking his clothes off to wash, tucking him into bed, indifferent to the stench as she grabbed a bucket to clean the mess.

"Let me help," his younger sister had asked, trying to take the sponge from Tori's hand.

She shook her head. "I'll do it. He's my husband." Her voice hitched as she said those words.

Wisely, his sister nodded and left the room, knowing it was a futile argument.

Tori whispered to the floor, "It's my mess."

When she finished, the floor was spotless. Tori walked into the bathroom, her hands shaking as she scrubbed her skin raw, unable to wash away the stain of the experience.

How did I get here? She remembered wondering, but Tori knew the answer.

He had been patient initially, waiting years to convince her to hang out. "Platonic, of course," he promised. "I'm not a bad guy. You're safe with me."

The following day, Tori was too hungover to remember more than a few clumsy kisses and shadowy images of laying across his bed.

"Where am I? Where are my clothes? Who the fuck is that?" she asked herself, peeking over at the form in the bed next to her. "Oh. Thank God I know his name."

He chose that moment to turn over. "Hi," Tori said tentatively, embarrassed at the position she'd found herself in.

"Morning. You were something special last night," he said, reaching a hand out to cup her bare breast.

"I was?" she flinched, putting two and two together.

He narrowed his eyes. "Yeah. You wanted it, remember?" He pulled the sheet away, exposing her nakedness to the chill of the air conditioner in his room.

"Well, I—" she started, the taste of cottonmouth making her choose her words with care. "I don't remember much." She called herself foul names in her head, ashamed of God knows what went on in that bed.

"Must've been one hell of a hangout," she chuckled, nervously fighting the urge to snatch the sheet from him. "This is embarrassing."

"Nah. You were good. Play your cards right, and you might be the perfect girl for me." He nodded sagely.

"You know what, imma show you." He got up and crossed the room to his dresser. Opening the top drawer, he dumped the contents on the floor. "Come back over tomorrow with a bag for the weekend. This is your drawer."

"Wow." Tori blinked in surprise. She searched for the right words to lighten the moment. "I don't remember what happened between us last night...but if I'm going to feel bad, I might as well do it again."

He grinned, climbing back into the bed.

What they had was complicated, fun, and unhealthy. It worked until it didn't.

The longer she had stayed, the more everything she liked about herself seemed to wither. Years later, Tori was still figuring out how to reassemble the pieces of herself that had fractured during the marriage. Tori had grown quieter as their years together rolled by, voluntarily stifling herself in his Shadow.

She told him that once and he was surprised. "You would be nothing without me," he warned Tori as he slammed the door to her bedroom, aka the basement. At that point, she'd chosen to sleep down there on an air mattress. Anything was better than lying awake at night next to him.

Was that harsh? Was he the worst husband ever? Probably not—she was alive, right? That had to count for something. It didn't matter that a crate full of medical files and the fading scars all over her body told an ugly story. The physical damage he did was the easiest part to get over. Internal scars were different.

It's not that she didn't try to leave him. She counted at least seven times that she had her bags packed and a new apartment picked out. Craig proposed right at the buzzer. He was good at that. People liked to say you didn't know someone until you married them. That's a lie. You never knew anyone until you looked them in the eye and told them you wanted a divorce.

She should've never married Craig. The signs were clear from the very beginning: the cheating, the fighting, the threats, and the back-to-back trips to the hospital. "You should tell the doctor you lost your antibiotics and get a dose for me. You don't want anyone else to know about this, do you? You think I'm bad? I don't know what the big deal is. I didn't give you anything that an antibiotic can't take care of! If you leave me, there's a lot worse out there. If you're lucky, you'll catch AIDS and die." He was an ignorant asshole, but getting those words out of her head was still hard. How could someone you loved wish the worst for you?

Embarrassed, Tori did as she was told, but she was stopped for a heart-to-heart chat with her doctor before leaving the office. Dr. Morgan had known her since she was eight and was genuinely concerned about her well-being. Embarrassed by the statistics about Black women and sexual trauma the doctor shared, Tori damn near ran out of the office. A few rounds of antibiotics later, Dr. Morgan shook her head when Tori announced her engagement. "Tori, are you sure you want to marry this man?"

Looking down at her ring, Tori thought of what he had inscribed inside its band: *Addicted to You*. She tried for a confident smile. "It'll all be fine. That's behind us. He promised."

Almost two years after leaving, Tori often revisited that moment. What if she had said no? Tori wished someone would ask that question again on her wedding day, but the moment never came. She tried not to wonder if Craig ever loved her in the first place. Had she been an easy, willing target for him? Yeah. Willing, at least, if not easy. The real question was, had she ever loved him, or had she settled from shame?

Looking back, they only discussed marriage when he spoke about his career goals. From the moment they met, Tori was a part of his plan. So much for that.

After she left, Tori had been afraid to even say hello to a man. Now she caught herself going on dates and swiping right to see if there were any redeeming qualities in the male species. Tori wasn't ready to give up hope, but her outlook had been bleak. Maybe she was an insecure man magnet.

"Stop thinking dark shit, Tori," she murmured aloud.

The flashbacks were exhausting. Tori felt like the veterans that used to hang out in front of her Grandmother's house, reliving their bravery in combat but flinching at the sound of a bottle being run over. Why did those thoughts and experiences come flooding back so quickly? Today's situation was not the same as years of a bad marriage. Gerard was not Craig. He was an indecisive, messy asshole, but he was not Craig. On to the next, right? Right!

She sighed and stared out the window, lost in her thoughts, while her driver sped down the F.D.R.

Spending all this damn money on Uber was an investment. No more sticky, filthy trains and people screaming "SHOWTIME!" while they backflipped their way through the crowded train car.

Imagine sitting down after a long ass day and getting kicked in the head 'cause some overzealous kid wanted to pole dance on the ceiling. It's not that Tori didn't love the experience, but sometimes you just wanted to get from point A to point B with no hassle…or train traffic. What the fuck was train traffic? How was that even a thing?

Seriously, Uber Black was the only way to go. There was nothing like a bona fide New York Uber driver with a 4.97 rating seamlessly weaving in and out of traffic. Tori believed that Uber drivers were a vital part of the N.Y. experience (along with the honorable mention—of drunk girls you met in bathrooms who tell you how much better you deserve in life). It was like they knew exactly what you needed. Want a therapist? They'd fill your trip with anecdotes and sage advice. Want a silent ride? They stare straight forward, never saying a word until it's time to get out of the car.

This one sensed her mood when she got in the car and turned on the radio to the strains of classic soul. "Water, lightning charger, more air?" he asked, returning to silence when she said no.

Someone asked what she needed for a change. How nice!

A rarity in her life after years of being the fixer for everyone else. Craig used to be chief on that list, manipulating her into doing whatever he wanted. Yet, Tori sat there year after year, willing to jump in like Captain Save' Em to clean up his messes. *Ride or Die, baby!*

She remembered how it started.

Tori walked into a dark apartment, tripping over a bottle of rum on the floor.

"Craig!" she cried, seeing him face down on the bed. Checking his breathing, she saw a half-empty bottle of Vicodin next to him.

Tori shook him. "How many did you take?!"

He stirred, mumbling something she couldn't understand.

"Craig!" her hands trembled as Tori searched the bed for his phone. "I'm calling 911!"

"Stop! You can't!" He shouted, grabbing her arm tightly. "I only took two. I'm good."

"Clearly you're not--" she pulled out of his grasp.

"They're kicking me out." He stumbled across the room, searching the floor for something.

Tori was confused. "I don't--"

Tossing an empty pizza box to the side, he found what he was looking for. "The school!" Craig thrust a letter toward her. "They're kicking me out."

"But how?" She scanned the letter. "You weren't going to class?"

"I missed a few." He picked up the bottle from the floor, taking a deep gulp.

Tori shook her head. "Baby...don't drink anymore."

"Might as well." He took another swig. "My mother's going to kill me."

Craig threw the bottle against the door, sending glass and liquor flying. His shoulders shook as he began to sob.

Tori ran to the bathroom to get paper towels. "The letter says you still have a chance to make up the work if you pass over the summer."

"I don't have the money for another semester, and catching up on the papers will take a miracle. I can't tell my mother about this." His forlorn expression got to her.

Craig was lucky his parents paid most of his tuition, but another semester might stretch the budget too tight. While his family wasn't particularly wealthy, his mother had made smart investments that allowed her to be their primary breadwinner and put her son through college.

Tori bent down, picking up pieces of broken glass from the floor. "I can help you," she offered, coming up with a plan. "We'll apply for a few scholarships, and I can help you with the essays."

"You?" he scoffed.

"Yeah." His tone made Tori second-guess herself for a moment. "It's worth a try. This is your dream. But you can't do this again." She shook the bottle of pills.

"Relax. I'm not going to O.D." He took the bottle away from her. "I had a headache."

She wasn't buying that. "I'm serious! They're willing to work with you." Tori sighed. "Don't throw that away by fucking up on purpose."

Craig studied her for a moment. "You'd do that for me?"

"Of course," Tori replied earnestly. She didn't want to see him stuck in the same spot she was, taking shitty jobs to pay the rent because she couldn't afford more than a couple of credits per year.

Craig grinned at her. "I love you."

Tori's eyes grew wide; it was the first time he had said it. "You do?" she asked.

Craig kissed her on the forehead. "Yeah. You're mine. This shit's kicking in again. I've gotta lay down." He pointed to the computer. "Think you can get started?"

Luckily for him, it worked. Tori filled that void for the next few years while he passed out drunk, high, or both. Craig would always start with flattery, feeding into her need to be needed. "But you're so much better at it than I am," he'd say.

After a while, they could only tolerate each other when they were wasted. It was hard to pinpoint the moment that changed, but she remembered praying for ways to keep the peace. Craig was a full-time job that, after a decade, Tori was happy to quit.

The very same things that attract you to a person could be the catalyst for jealousy. He took pride in flaunting her in front of his friends and bosses but resented when she got more attention than he did. Grey hair aside, Tori looked younger now that she had left him. As her Grandma used to say, "Black don't crack unless it's on crack."

He masked his low self-esteem in designer clothes Tori had to foot the bill for and cars he couldn't afford to lease. She never understood how someone could be flashy and cheap simultaneously. An emotional sadist, he enjoyed roasting her in public past the point of taking it far. A small part of her knew it was lies and manipulation, but the phrases he used were the same ones Tori had heard about herself at her mother's knees. She thanked God for reserving that small space within her because believing the horrible things he would say was the dumbest shit she could've done. For a motherfucker who played mind games, you would think he'd at least be some sex god, but nope. Craig was shaped like a thick-ass prickly pear and was a lackluster lover at best.

The worse shape he was in, the more psychologically abusive he became. One of his favorite pastimes was befriending people to ridicule them. Whenever Tori asked him to stop, Craig redirected his efforts her way. He had a way of twisting an argument. "I could break you if I wanted to," he taunted her.

She justified his words until there was nothing but bitterness left between them.

Tori swallowed her pain, allowing her rage to build until all she could do was scream. Craig relished those moments, picking away at her carefully, deliberately crowding her until she'd fight desperately to get away, and then playing the victim.

She'd hang her head in shame, picking up broken glass from the photo frames on the wall, apologizing to the neighbors for the noise.

"Miss, you should just leave him," said one well-meaning neighbor. Embarrassed, Tori walked away without a word.

"Nosy bitch!" he said as she closed the door.

"Nosy bitch…" Tori repeated quietly, wishing she could take the advice.

Craig never remembered all he'd done to provoke her, but she was always in the wrong for reacting. Craig would answer, "This is your fault. You always want to live in the past," whenever she would call him out.

"My fault?" her voice rose shrilly. "You threw me into a fucking metal frame and made me walk to the hospital!"

"But you came back..." the voice in her head would say.

That November night had been nuts. Tori's arm had swollen badly after their fight over her choice to visit her dad instead of spending time with his family. Craig hated when she couldn't be his arm candy.

"I don't want to go. Last time, your mother lied and told her sister that I have an eating disorder," she said. Tori was furious when it happened, but out of respect, she decided to let him handle it. To her disgust, Craig laughed it off. "She knows it's not true. You're getting fat." He chose to say nothing to his mother.

"You're going," Craig pulled a t-shirt on. "Stop being a bitch and get dressed."

Tori scoffed and walked past him to go to the living room, but he caught her by the arm. "You're going to go, and you aren't going to embarrass me," he hissed.

"Nigga, get your fuckin' hands off me," Tori growled back.

"What Bitch!" He grabbed her throat and slammed her head into the wall.

Tori fought free, grabbing everything in reach to throw at him so she could escape. His eyes went completely black when she clipped him on the cheek with an apple-shaped bottle of Lolita Lempicka. Craig choke-slammed her into their metal bed frame as she begged him to stop. When he was finished, Tori lay on the floor, too stunned to cry.

Trying to get up, she found that one of her arms could barely move. "I think I need to go to the hospital." She hiccuped, refusing the tears that wanted to fall.

"You'll figure it out." Craig watched her struggle for a bit before grabbing his keys.

He touched the spot where the bottle hit him. "Stupid bitch! Now you'll miss dinner."

Craig looked at her in disgust before slamming the door behind him.

Unable to put it on alone, Tori clutched her coat to her chest and walked to the hospital in misty 40-degree weather.

"We've checked the x-ray. It's not broken, but you have contusions and a possible hairline fracture. Your arm will be sore for a while." The emergency room doctor looked up from her clipboard. "Is this from a domestic incident? Are you safe in your home?"

"I fell. I'm safe." The lie rolled off her tongue too quickly. The doctor sighed, making a note in her chart.

When Tori got home hours later, Craig stood in their living room with leftovers in his hand and tears in his eyes.

"You can't leave me! We've been through so much together. Nobody else would understand." He looked at her arm, dangling awkwardly in a hospital-issued sling, and laughed. "You didn't even need to go to the hospital. There's nothing wrong with you. I only hit you to shut you up."

Tori refused to call the police. Sending a Black man to jail was the furthest thing from her mind. Things would get better. They had to. He was under a lot of pressure to succeed. Tori did her best to get comfortable with apologizing and overcompensating for what he did. His friends who saw the fighting shook it off as passion, but she never forgot the pity that crossed their faces at her excuses.

One night, on the rare occasion Craig allowed her to have her friends over, two of them saw Craig dragging her across the floor. They jumped up, ready to beat his ass, but she insisted Craig was playing. She didn't want anyone going to jail for fighting her battles.

Was it healthy? Nope, arguably not. Ten years later, Tori was still treading water on the deep side of the pool. Despite her efforts to move forward, there was always fear in her mind. How would he hurt her next? Craig had been erratic ever since they started the divorce process. The latest bit of ridiculousness was his asking for joint custody and visitation of the cats. He hated caring for them for the entire time they were together.

This was just another mind game.

Chapter 3

The First Stone

The car arrived at Leslie's apartment building. Tori used her key, taking a moment to appreciate the latest renovations in the lobby. The building was an old office space converted into multi-floor luxe private residences. Wealthy, even by New York standards, Leslie's family kept the home for their sporadic visits to the U.S. each year. It was a no-brainer that their daughter would live there when they allowed her to "find herself" before they chose the trajectory of her life for her. Their section was a massive penthouse loft with a domed skylight and rooftop access. As if that wasn't enough, its north-facing floor-to-ceiling windows gave lucky onlookers an unobstructed view of Central Park.

The image of Leslie's father saying, "Everything the light touches…" while holding her up in the window like a Caucasian infant Simba popped into Tori's mind unbidden. She giggled. Waking up to views like this was a sign that generational wealth should be everyone's goal.

Growing up, Tori's parents worked hard to ensure their daughter attended the best schools they could afford, drilling into her that the world would make her work for every inch of space she took up.

To help make ends meet, her mother schlepped her around the country for talent shows, the prize money contributing to paying household bills. Tori sat by the window watching children play outside while she was forced to memorize scripts. A career was a heavy burden for a three-year-old, but failure was not an option, and she was expected to win every award. They would travel far for long weekends of rehearsals, getting home on Monday mornings at 2 am. A few hours later, Tori would sit in class, unable to reconcile the strange adult-like schedule that set her apart from the kids around her. Her mother set a rule to promote normalcy—if she wasn't performing, bedtime was at 4 pm. Tori didn't have to be asleep by then, but the consequences for not being dressed for bed were high. Hindsight made that the likely cause of her adult insomnia.

When puberty hit, money troubles began to plague the family, making her parents' relationship unmendable. They moved to a cheaper area—Hood-adjacent, the type of neighborhood that chewed you up and spat you out if you were soft. Already isolated, she couldn't play outside because of the high probability of getting jumped or shot. She learned the hard way.

A bunch of kids cornered her in an alley once, pelting her head with heavy rocks and chunks of concrete until Tori escaped. A biblical style stoning. The reason behind the attack; winning an award at school. That was the final straw for her father. He came home the next day with a small pair of steel-toed boots and taught her to throw a punch. Every day for months, he trained her until she could knock him down, forging a deeper bond with his daughter through adversity. Not that they needed one. Behind closed doors, their world fell apart as her parents struggled to keep up appearances.

Tori would watch her mother hang up her beautiful mink coat in the closet, take off her diamonds, and carefully remove the makeup from her face by candlelight because they had no electricity. It was fun in the summer when the days were long and the nights were warm. Every day they ate boiled lima beans and corn they kept packed between 5lb bags of ice in the cooler. Can't have a refrigerator with no power. In the winter, she sat on the floor in front of the oven to thaw her fingers, praying for Christmas miracles but waking up to screams. The family car had been repossessed overnight with everything in it. It was also Tori's birthday. What a gift.

By the time she was a teenager, their anger toward each other became twisted into a test of her loyalty. Tori stayed with her mother. Not that she had a choice. Every night her mother locked them together to sleep in Tori's twin-sized bed. Her father was only allowed to hug her goodnight before being barricaded on the other side of the house like a criminal.

Before the split, they sent her down south on the premise of a summer theater workshop. Two weeks into the program, her mother showed up. "I've left your father. We're never going to live with him again. Also, your grandmother's funeral was nice. Don't cry. She wouldn't have wanted you there." Tori was crushed.

Now a single-parent household, her mother made it clear that her way was the only way, and the thought of telling her no meant an ass-whooping for betrayal. Her father tried to shield her from the worst while they were together but escaped for his sanity. It didn't matter now. The past was the past.

Tori was turning thirty soon, and with her own failed marriage under her belt, Tori understood them more than ever.

The elevator door opened, bringing her back to the present.

Plastering a smile across her face, Tori walked in.

"Hey, Lady! Where are you?" she called out, trying to figure out which part of the massive four-bedroom, five-bathroom loft to explore.

"Hey, Babe!" Leslie's voice echoed from the master bathroom. "Perfect timing. We should pregame, then go for food and maybe some dancing. Fuck boys! Who needs them?"

"We do! But mostly for sex." Tori shouted. "Then they can return to whatever hell they came from."

"Exactly!" Leslie ran out of the bathroom, toweling her hair dry. "Babe, it's going to be OK. If you decide you'd rather stay in and cry it out at any point, we will. I'll make tea, and we can watch T.V. I've got a list of your favorite movies to cheer you up. We can watch the one about the groove."

Tori grunted as Leslie charged into her with the hug that, deep down, she needed. "I'm not heartbroken; I'm pissed. Wait—The Emperor's New Groove or How Stella Got Her Groove Back?" Tori raised an eyebrow. She wiggled out of the hug. "I shouldn't have introduced you to either."

"No!" Leslie screeched. "It's my new favorite. All white people watch is The Notebook! And the actor was so hot."

Tori chuckled. "I need some water first." She grabbed a bottle and the drink Leslie had left for her from the fridge.

"OK," Leslie returned to the bathroom to finish getting ready. "I'll throw some makeup on my face, and then we're out the door."

Drink in hand, Tori faced the window, trying to banish the uneasy feeling in her stomach. *Get it together, girl.*

Leslie entered the room wearing a satin dress and a pair of dingy converses. Mismatched-chic. She grabbed her purse. "Let's go downstairs. Uber is on its way."

Tori debated changing her clothes but decided against it. It didn't matter; she would have looked like Black Orphan Annie with Leslie's outfit on.

"Maybe it's the long legs..." she mused as they left.

Chapter 4

Mind Control

They walked into Thai Mi Up, a hole-in-the-wall pre-party staple in the West Village. The place was famous for its all-day happy hour and generously greasy portions of Pad Thai at questionably low prices. Was the chicken fresh? No. Was the wine great? Also, no, but you were treated like family as soon as you walked in.

Their favorite waiter, Hu, always ensured they had the best table in the house, a corner spot with four seats, a rickety heater overhead, and excellent selfie lighting. You could walk in with twenty dollars and leave with two entrees, three appetizers, and an entire bottle of wine.

Thai Mi Up was the perfect place to begin your evening with people-watching while staying central to all the hottest spots to party.

Tori grabbed the menu, pretending to read it closely.

"Why bother?" Leslie said. "You order the same thing every time."

"You never know when they're going to update the menu. We asked for spicy rice so much that they added it because of us," Tori reminded her.

"I just don't understand." Leslie blurted out. "I didn't like him anyway, but why would he stand you up? Did something happen?"

Tori shook her head, taking a sip of the merlot that Hu had brought over. "Nope. He gave me a song and dance, then changed his mind. He told me he's not ready and will call me next week."

"Yeah, but you didn't want to date him anyway," Leslie said.

"Yeah. Maybe I was a little flattered. My ego liked being the exception to his 'no feelings rule.' Gerard isn't my problem. Half the time, I feel numb. Craig probably broke something in me." She took an aggressive bite of shrimp toast.

"You don't mean that!" Leslie exclaimed, causing a few curious people to eyeball them.

Tori put her head in her hands. "I know. I don't know why I said that. I'm having mood swings. Right before Gerard stood me up, I found out Craig had updated the divorce papers to ask for alimony. "

"WHAT?! But he's the one with money. How are you going to pay him? He's an accountant, for God's sake!" Leslie half-shouted. Time in the U.S. was rubbing off on her. Leslie's prim and proper parents would've been horrified at the idea of a raised tone in public view.

"I know." Tori shook her head angrily. "Craig wants half of my money and visitation of the cats. He doesn't even like cats. He's fucking with me. Honestly, I don't even care about Gerard canceling. I'm tired of forcing myself to be the bigger person. It's like every man I meet is fucked up. I'm over this shit."

Hu interrupted, setting another appetizer on the table. "Ladies, this one is on the house."

They smiled their thanks.

"I sold him almost all the furniture I had just bought. I redecorated it so it wouldn't look like I had ever lived there. I'm a great ex. I leave you the fuck alone. I never even reported him to the police, yet he tries to fuck with me at every opportunity." Tori's frustrated tears threatened to fall.

Noticing, Leslie passed her a clean tissue. "For a man who tried to paint you as a golddigger, your ex can't stop demanding things from you. Don't worry; it will be over soon. You said it before. It's character-building. If he wants half, laugh at him. He won't get away with it."

Tori laughed. "I'm not enough of a character already? I was on my way to your house wondering if he ever loved me. At all?" She sighed. "That man used every tool at his disposal to break me down. Craig knew what he was doing. I've made so many excuses for him. I've got to stop pretending like he didn't tell me that this is what he does to people."

"What are you talking about?" Leslie asked.

Tori leaned back in her chair with a sigh. "The worst part is that this isn't the first time he's done something like this. Craig plays this game with everyone. I thought he was joking when he said he was a sociopath until it was too late. Shit, he told me his exes ended up in a psych ward after dating him. My dumb ass took it as a joke. I really believed that shit wouldn't happen to me. The moment I moved in, he would tell me how he would break me if I tried to leave."

Leslie hugged her. "It's going to be OK. He won't get away with it."

"We both know he probably will." Tori sighed. "Craig prepared me for everything he's putting me through now. It will all be over one day, but this shit hurts."

Leslie waved Hu over. "Well, we will have a great night. No Craig's or Gerard's allowed. There must be a non-stressful man in New York! It would help if you had some fun. Cut loose. Renee, the girl I was supposed to meet, just texted me. She's in the area. She's sweet. You'll like her. Let's have her stop by, and if you aren't feeling it, we can ditch her and go home."

Tori nodded. For the most part, Leslie's friends were a lot of fun.

At her nod, Leslie squealed, sending Renee the address.

Tori changed the subject. "Anyway, how is the job search going?"

"I haven't booked a gig in weeks, and my parents are giving me hell again. How they manage from 4,000 miles away, I'll never understand." Leslie groaned. "Maybe we should take shots for this."

"What if you worked at my job? The pay wouldn't be great, but you can make great connections. Let me talk to Paris." Tori offered.

Leslie laughed. "I love you, but I'll pass. Every time we talk about that place, you get a wrinkle on your forehead, and that guy you work with found me on Facebook and asked me to be a nude model."

"Touché. He's a creep. Well, at least a job can delay the process of leaving." Tori raised an eyebrow. "Unless you're pining for home. You should butter your dad up and convince him to let you work for his company."

"That's the worst-case scenario. Not at all. I've never felt so much at home as I do here. Besides, I can't leave you. If everything else fails, I'll marry you, and we can be best friends living happily ever after." Leslie batted her eyelashes.

Tori rolled her eyes. "Asking me to defraud the government might be the sweetest thing to happen to me all day. But don't say that too loud; my mother's gaydar will go off."

"Never say never." Leslie winked. Her phone chirped. "She's on her way."

Chapter 5

Three's Company

"So, tell me about her," Tori asked.

"I met her at a modeling agency I'm trying to work with," Leslie answered. "She's originally from Ireland and is here for an ad campaign her company wants her to lead. We've gone out for coffee a few times. I think she's just looking for new friends. I'm hoping I can get her to put me on something long-term."

A tall, curvy redhead made a beeline for them as she finished talking. Leslie stood up with a smile. "Tori, this is Renee. Renee, this is my best friend I told you about. Thanks for coming."

Hu came over with water, an extra wine glass, and a table setting for their new guest.

Renee smiled. "I've heard so many wonderful things about you from Lez— I already know you. She told me you give the best advice!"

Leslie nodded, "Tori has been like a sister to me since we met."

"Aww, it's nice to meet you." Tori never knew how to respond to compliments anymore- years of conditioning had made her first reaction to meeting new people to be either nervousness or silence. Something else to add to the list of things she needed to work on. "We were drinking merlot, but we can order something else if you'd like."

"No, that's perfect. I could use a glass. It's been a long day." Renee smiled. "I was looking forward to meeting you. Leslie said you're getting divorced. I told my husband I was here for work but need to meet with an attorney. I want a divorce too."

Tori froze, pinning Leslie with a glare that said, "How could you?" She wasn't ashamed of getting divorced, but it was her story to tell, and Leslie knew that. Regardless, now was not the time to have that discussion.

Tori exhaled quietly. "I'm still in the thick of it, but if you have any questions I can answer, I'll tell you what I know. Number one tip, they are capitalizing on one of the biggest decisions of your life. Pick one who isn't going to try to fuck you. They don't make money if you change your mind."

She sat back in her chair, signaling Hu to refill her glass of water.

"I never loved my husband," said Renee. "This was an easy decision."

That was a surprising thing to admit to a stranger. Tori quirked an eyebrow. "You went through with the wedding anyway, though?"

"My family said I had to," she said.

Tori nodded. She had tried to do the same after a fight with Craig a few days before her own.

It was hard enough to leave a marriage, but doing it while moving to a new country took courage. Tori reserved her initial impression of Renee's gaffe as tacky but unintentional.

I'll let it go, she thought.

Leslie proposed a toast. "To new friends and a great evening!"

The women clinked their glasses and called for more food.

"So," Renee leaned toward Tori, "Are you seeing anyone now?"

"Not anymore," said Tori as Leslie snickered into her glass.

"I downloaded a few apps since I've been here," said Renee.

Leslie nodded. "I'm dating a few guys from one."

Tori rolled her eyes. "I'm going to give those a break. I'm tired of swiping for a new fuckboy du jour." The thought of running into another Gerard made her want to throw her phone.

"I love it. I've traveled worldwide, but New York has the hottest men," said Renee. "I've only been here a month, and I've had more sex than I did with my husband. Last night I hooked up with this male model. He did some blow and popped a Viagra. We had sex all night. Best

41

dick I've ever had."

"Was it the one you showed me a picture of?" asked Leslie.

"No." Renee sighed. "I keep calling him. I think he's ghosting me."

Yep. This girl is definitely tacky, she thought, listening to Renee's story as Leslie expertly avoided her eyes.

Two hours and a bottle of wine later, the three stood outside, considering what to do next. Taking a poll, they decided to walk around the neighborhood and bar-hop.

"Wait! Let's take a picture first," Leslie said. She called out to a couple waiting to cross the street. "Excuse me! Can you take our photo?"

Smiling awkwardly, Tori leaned in for a group shot.

"Thank you!" Leslie called out. She inspected the pictures closely. "Not bad. They framed us well. Let's go this way. There are a bunch of bars with decent music."

Tori yawned, fighting the urge to go home. "I'm cool with us going to another bar. I don't want to go too crazy tonight. It took me three days to recover last time, and you missed your flight."

Renee said, "It's Saturday, Tori. We've all had a long week, so let's have fun."

Chapter 6

Kak Dela

They wandered around until they saw a nightclub with a line wrapped around the corner. To the side of the door, a thick cloud of cigar smoke hovered around a group of tall men in sharp suits.

Renee's sea-green eyes locked in on one of them as they passed. She elbowed Tori and Leslie. "Do you see him?" She nodded toward a particularly tall blond one. "He looks like that actor. We should say hi."

"What's our pickup line?" asked Leslie, pursing her lips.

"Girl, introduce yourself," Tori said, rolling her eyes.

"I'll sound silly. You do it," Leslie pleaded.

"No Craig's, no Gerard's, remember?" Tori reminded her, but a pout was forming on her friend's face.

"Forget it...excuse me!" Tori called out. The men paused their smoking, looking at the three women. "Good evening. Is there a cigar bar near here?"

The tall one spoke first, his heavy Russian accent and tone direct. "No. We brought our own."

He sized them up. "You're all pretty. Come inside to our party."

Tori felt it was less of an invitation and more of an order. He didn't look like the type used to being turned down.

Immediately wary, Tori blurted out. "No. That's OK. We were just curious." She glanced back at her friends, realizing they had both been flanked by the men standing near the blond.

The blond stepped forward. "I'm Andrei."

Tori shook his hand reluctantly. "It's nice to meet you, but we should really be going."

Andrei lifted an eyebrow. "Without them?"

Tori looked back, only to see Leslie and Renee already dancing into the nightclub.

See, this is that white bullshit, Tori thought.

Groaning aloud, she pulled out her phone and sent her other best friend, Aaliyah, a message, "If I go missing, I was with Leslie. Also, Craig and Gerard both tried the fuck out of me today. I'll call you in the morning. Love you!"

Even though they never met in person, Aaliyah was not Leslie's biggest fan. "I don't trust her" had become her mantra. Regardless, they had a rule, always send an update if your plans changed.

She put her phone in her pocket and hurried through the nightclub, ready to drag Leslie out of there. When the door closed behind her, Tori was hit with heavy EDM beats and a crowd of flailing, sweaty people.

How ironic that the DJ chose that moment to scream into the microphone, "RUSSIAN MAFIA IN THE BUILDING!"

Mafia? Tori thought. *"What the fuck? Oh, hell no!"*

She looked back toward the exit and saw Andrei trailing closely behind her, nodding at someone she couldn't see. The crowd parted like the Red Sea, making way for a line of men carrying four tables and chairs. Like magic, oysters, a rack of lamb, bottles of vodka, a mountain of caviar, and a seafood tower were placed on the table. It was Beauty and the Beast, minus sassy furniture singing "Be Our Guest."

"Now, THIS is service!" she thought.

Leslie and Renee grinned at each other as they settled down at the table. Andrei pulled out Tori's chair before sitting down himself.

Leaning over, she whispered to Leslie, "One drink, and then we're out of here."

"Relax," Leslie said. "We're just saying hi. They're cute. Loosen up."

Andrei skimmed his hand across Tori's back. "Try this," he said. His authoritative tone slightly grated Tori's nerves as he poured a shot for her. "This is Russian vodka. Nothing like that crap they sell in stores."

"*Spasibo*," Tori said as they clinked glasses.

Andrei was startled. "You know Russian?"

"A bit," she said. "I learned it as a child."

"I've never met...." Andrei paused and looked at her thoughtfully, "...a Black girl who could speak my language."

Noting the pause, Tori smiled sarcastically. "Surprise!"

Turning away, she focused on her friends. This was not the first time someone reacted with shock to her knowing another language. Her mother used to get a kick out of Tori speaking Russian and Mandarin to her clients. She hadn't remembered more than a few sentences in either language in years.

Everyone grabbed a glass to take their share. Renee and Leslie grimaced as they threw back their shots and looked at her expectantly.

With a sigh, Tori tossed hers back. "When in Rome..."

Chapter 7

All The Girls Standing in Line for the Bathroom

"*This place isn't that bad,*" Tori thought.

The music was so loud she swore she could see the sound waves as Leslie and Renee danced with their new friends. Tori could barely catch anyone's name unless they shouted. So far, she had only learned that this crew was ready to party. The shortest of the bunch, Ivan, had already taken five shots and was intensely focused on grinding against Renee's leg.

Speaking of shots, she wondered, how many are they planning on pouring? She glanced around, noticing that everyone was getting drunk very quickly. Tori had agreed to one but allowed them to refill her glass a second time.

Ivan walked over, shouting drunkenly, "I'm going to dance with you." He grabbed a chair, awkwardly twerking for her with party sparklers shooting from his mouth. She laughed, applauding the performance.

Renee and Leslie cheered from the dance floor. If Tori was enjoying herself, those two were having an absolute blast. At one point, she'd seen the guys hoist them in the air to "Hava Nagila." Enjoying the loose party atmosphere, she felt the tension leaving her body. Maybe Leslie was right.

Realizing she needed to go to the restroom, Tori squeezed through the crowd to tell them where she was going.

"Look after each other," she told them. "I'll be right back." They nodded and went back to their revelry.

"How long is this fucking line?" she thought. *"Twenty minutes and at least fifteen girls are still ahead of me. If it weren't for the fact that I have to pee, I'd make Renee and Leslie leave right now."*

This place was too crowded. Feeling dizzy and hot, Tori leaned against the sticky wall and closed her eyes.

"I love your hair," a heavily accented voice said in her ear.

Startled, Tori opened her eyes and saw a blonde woman staring at her. "Thank you," she answered.

Her eyes narrowed and glittered strangely under the strobe lights. "How did you come here? There aren't that many girls like you at this party," she asked.

Oh fuck. Something about white women saying "girl" made her hair stand on end.

It's been a good night. Lord, please don't let her test me. Tori weighed her options, choosing not to respond. She counted the line again; seven women left. *Thank God! I don't have that many kegels left in me. I want to go home.*

The longer she waited, the more the music thumped in her chest. How did she get so drunk? She needed to go to the bathroom, get her friends, and leave.

Just in time, it was her turn. Tori stumbled into the restroom, trying not to pitch over in the darkness of the stall.

A little more water when she got back to the table, and she would be fine. *Pee, flush, rinse your face, and go collect those two,* she told herself.

She took a deep breath and walked out of the stall to wash her hands. As she glanced into the mirror, Tori saw that the blonde from the line was still watching her.

"Long night, huh?" the woman said with a closed mouth smile.

Tori nodded, not wanting to be drawn into a conversation, "Excuse me." She stepped past her and made her way back to the table, but no one was there.

Everyone was probably on the dance floor since she had stood in the line for a while, so Tori sat down, helping herself to a closed bottle of water from the table.

A few minutes later, she saw Ivan walking toward the exit.

"Hey! Have you seen my friends?" she called out.

He blinked at her in confusion before saying, "Oh, they left and went to another party. Come. We can go to them now."

He reached for her hand, but Tori pulled away. "What do you mean they left?" She raised her voice. "My friends would never leave me."

Ivan looked around them and walked off.

Well, that's bullshit. Tori thought. *Let me walk around and find them.*

As she pushed through the crowd, Tori felt like the room was closing in on her. The lights seemed brighter, swirling instead of flashing. A cacophony pulsed around her. What was happening? Her heart raced. Where were they?

Panicked, she stood still in the middle of the dance floor and screamed over the music, "Leslie! Renee! Have you seen my friends?"

She pushed and grabbed anyone she could reach, trying to find them. Leslie wouldn't desert her. *Would she?* All Tori wanted was to find someone who knew them and could tell her where they had gone.

Something was wrong.

Why was her speech slurred? It was getting harder and harder to focus. Tori felt like she was dragging her feet.

She felt someone grab her arm but could barely lift her head to register who was holding her.

The night air hit her face, bringing more focus to the scene. She was outside now. Turning her head, she saw she was being carried between two huge bouncers. The fuck?

She tried again, "Where are my friends?" To her ears, her words sounded garbled. *They probably think I'm drunk.*

The bouncers propped Tori up against the building and walked away to break up a fight that had formed in front of the club doors.

Willing herself to move her hands, she slid them into her pockets. Shit! Her coat was inside. At least she had her phone. Tori looked at the phone to unlock it and realized it wasn't hers.

Her last coherent thought was, *I think I switched my phone with Renee's.* She had the same one.

The next thing she knew, Tori realized someone had covered her with a blazer and wrapped their arms around her.

"I've got you," he said. It was Andrei.

"Whaa happ?" she slurred.

Somehow, Andrei understood. "I'll take you to your friend's house. Where does she live?"

Tori stared at him blankly. "I...I can't memb...Central Park ..." With her muddled memory, she could only remember the general area of Leslie's house. Her head was reeling. Tori closed her eyes.

What time is it? She felt weak and confused. *I don't have any of my stuff. My ID, phone, and keys are all in my coat pocket. Oh my God! Renee's phone is gone! When did that happen?*

Andrei let go of her and stepped into the street, leaving her reeling without his support. A yellow taxicab pulled up.

They never stop for me, she noted. Taking charge, he ushered her in, getting in next to her. The sensation of the moving car rocked her to sleep.

Andrei gently nudged her awake. "I'm going to get you a hotel room. You need water and rest."

Tori opened her eyes and protested weakly. "No."

"I'm not going to hurt you." Andrei laughed. "I'm getting you a room to sleep it off."

Unable to respond, Tori closed her eyes and leaned her head against the cool glass of the window. In what felt like seconds, they pulled up to the hotel.

Andrei spoke to the concierge, quickly obtaining a room key. He led her into the elevator with one arm wrapped around her waist and the other holding her arm like a debutante. He opened the door to a large suite with two queen-sized beds on the top floor. Scooping her up like a bride, Andrei gently placed her on the bed.

Struggling to keep her eyes open, Tori rolled over, murmuring into the pillow. "Don't get any ideas…" before passing out.

Chapter 8

Rock and a Hard Place

Tori woke up in a very unfamiliar setting with a pounding headache and cottonmouth.

Where the hell am I? she wondered. She looked around the room, realizing that she was in a hotel.

A déjà vu moment. The last time she blacked out like that, Tori woke up in a relationship with Craig.

At least this time, she was still fully dressed.

He didn't touch me. Thank God.

Tori glanced over at the other bed where Andrei was sleeping. She took in as many details as she could. In the dim hotel light, he was better looking than Tori'd realized. With his suit jacket casually thrown across a chair at the end of the bed, she noticed his shirt was unbuttoned at the collar, revealing a pendant on a delicate chain. Could she sneak past him? He was at least 250 lbs with a well-muscled frame and darkened knuckles. A fighter. He wouldn't be easy to overpower.

As if he could read her mind, Andrei opened his eyes. "How do you feel?" he asked.

Tori croaked out. "What the hell happened?"

Andrei sat up and sighed. "The men with me were planning on keeping you and your friends."

"FUCK you mean keep us?" Tori growled. Her mind immediately went to Dateline's specials about trafficking victims.

Be smart, Tori.

The view from the hotel window proved that she was still in New York. What was his plan?

He shrugged. "It happens. Sometimes girls go out for a good time, and they recruit them for the company."

"I didn't see a job application!" Tori's eyes darted around the room for something to hit him if necessary. She clumsily propped herself up on the bed. "You motherfuckers wanted to sell us!" Tori was furious but knew lashing out would only worsen things. She needed him on her side. Tori pulled the covers against herself, noting how weak her hands still felt.

He crossed from his bed to hers. "I wasn't going to let them have you," he said earnestly. "You were different. I knew that when we spoke outside."

This was too much. Tori tried to get out of bed, but dizziness and nausea hit her.

Andrei grabbed her hand. "Hey...lay down."

She looked at the clock on the nightstand. 4 am. *Shit!*

Rationally, Tori knew that she should get the fuck out of there, but where could she go? With no money, coat, phone, keys, or ID, she ran the risk of running into the same type of people or worse if she left. She considered calling 911, but with her slurred speech, they would probably find some reason to arrest or blame her for what happened. Tori couldn't even remember a phone number for anyone she knew to come to get her.

Hell, if I can't get out of bed, how will I walk around in the street?

She swallowed her fear, choosing her words carefully. "I'm grateful that you've helped me. I still really don't feel well. I need to close my eyes for a little longer, and then I'll be out of your hair."

Andrei's face dropped. "The room is yours, Tori. I'm just here to make sure you get back to them safely. Nothing is going to happen to you."

For some reason, she believed him.

Lord, protect me, please, she prayed, losing the battle to stay awake.

Tori woke up, feeling the pressure of an arm wrapped around her. Looking over her shoulder, she saw Andrei sleeping next to her.

What in the hell is happening here? She wondered, trying to extricate herself. He shifted in his sleep, pulling her in closer. Tori felt something poking her in her back. *Oh God, What is that!?* She hoped that he had picked up a banana at some point.

If it weren't for the fact that he ran with sex traffickers, this would feel really nice. Too nice. She hadn't woken up being held in years. A sound in between a laugh and sob slipped out as the absurdity of her predicament hit her, but this was not the time to give into the nervous breakdown the situation deserved. She stifled the noise, feeling his arms tighten around her in response.

Sensing a change in his breathing, Tori peeked over her shoulder. Andrei stared at her intently.

Lovely eyes, she thought. Before she could say a word, he kissed her.

Tori froze. What should she do? Even if he wasn't in charge, Andrei was at least aware of what their plans for her were, but he had helped facilitate her escape and probably saved her life.

Her mind raced as Andrei clung to her.

Chapter 9

Lost & Found

Tori buttoned her shirt in the bathroom mirror. There would be a very serious self-reckoning for everything that had happened in the past twenty-four hours. She needed to get out of this room and find Leslie.

Taking a deep breath, she opened the bathroom door. "Andrei...I need to get to Leslie's apartment."

"Let's go to breakfast first?" Andrei asked with a sly expression on his face. He didn't seem ready to get out of bed.

Blushing, Tori stared at her feet. "No, I really need to find them. What time is it?" she asked.

"I know a good restaurant not far from here. It's open. We can stop before we go to her place," Andrei said.

There were many reasons to say no, but her main one was a concern for Leslie. It still made no sense how they were separated.

"I'm not going to be able to eat yet. Let's find them first, and then we can all get something together," she said. In her mind, it was a compromise.

Sighing, he threw off the covers and dressed.

"Can I borrow your phone again?" she asked. He nodded, tossing it her way.

Access denied again. Damn, strong passwords. Tori had grown so dependent upon her phones and computer that she never took the time to memorize anyone's number. She would have called Leslie, but her phone was an international number, and Tori didn't even know Renee's last name. She said a silent prayer that they were fine.

Twenty minutes later, Tori and Andrei walked out of the hotel. In the morning light, she realized they were only a couple of blocks away from Leslie's.

Tori hurried in the direction of the house while Andrei trailed behind her. She ran at the sight of Leslie's building.

Shit! The front door was locked, and the doorman wasn't in the lobby. Tori rang the bell, praying that someone was there to answer.

"It's me! Let me in!" she shouted.

The door buzzed, and Tori hurried upstairs.

The three women jumped over each other when the door opened, everyone speaking simultaneously.

"Where were you? What happened? Are you OK?" Leslie asked.

"I was so worried about you. Renee, I lost your phone," Tori answered.

"You had my phone? Did you have my bag? Well, I lost my backpack, too," Renee said. "But where have you been all this time?"

Tori looked over her shoulder and saw Andrei standing behind her.

Tori cleared her throat. "I was at a hotel."

"A hotel?" Leslie and Renee looked at her in confusion.

"That doesn't matter." Tori changed the subject. "Why did you disappear? I went to the bathroom, and when I came back, you were gone."

Leslie and Renee looked at each other before casting a glance toward Andrei.

"Do you want to talk about this with him here?" Leslie said in a stage whisper.

Tori nodded. "He helped me when I couldn't find you. I blacked out. I don't even know how that happened."

Outside, the sound of an ambulance passing by stirred something in the back of her mind, but it faded before she could grasp it. Her head was still pounding.

Noticing her grimace, Leslie led Tori to the couch. "You're not well. Let's sit down."

"I'll get you some water," Renee added, grabbing a bottle from the kitchen.

Chapter 10

Puzzle Box

Renee walked to the couch. "Do you remember going to the bathroom while we were dancing?"

Tori nodded. "I shouldn't have left you alone."

"No. It was fine at first," Leslie said. "Ivan pulled us onto the table and started grabbing bottles off the bar. Security probably would've thrown us out if his friends hadn't stopped him. We aren't sure when but I started feeling nauseous, and Renee fell."

Tori glanced at Andrei to see his reaction and found him doing the same to her. *Motherfucker.* Tori chuckled darkly. "I can't believe this."

"Well," Renee continued, "Ivan said you wanted to go to another party and were waiting for us. They had already taken our coats and bags. We followed them to the car, but you weren't there."

Renee pointed to a red bruise on her arm. "Some of them tried to push us into the car, but we fought them off. Leslie managed to grab her bag and coat, but I didn't. We ran a few streets over until a cab stopped. The driver had to help us inside."

Tori looked at Andrei again. He was standing half shrouded in the shadow of the doorway, his face unreadable.

Tori shook her head. "Apparently, they were planning on selling us."

"Selling us? Like Taken?" Renee shouted, turning her fury toward him.

"Not now!" Tori said. Screaming at Andrei would make their already bad situation even worse.

With a pointed look toward the girls, she continued, "As soon as I got back to the table, Ivan told me that you guys had left too. I tried to search for you, but I must've blacked out. At some point, I realized that the phone in my pocket was yours, but I can't remember losing it. I'm so sorry. My only clear memory is Andrei getting a room because I couldn't remember my address or how to get here."

"We've got your phone," they said in unison.

"You do! Thank God! I called it this morning! Why didn't you answer?" Tori asked in confusion.

"Technically, we only have your wallet, but we'll get the phone today. The man who answered said that he'd meet us. We've been speaking to him this entire time," Renee replied.

"Thank you, God," Tori sighed in relief.

"Also, I knew you didn't have my phone. It's in Brooklyn," Renee said.

"Brooklyn? How'd it get out there?" Tori asked.

"It's still on, but nobody's answering," Renee stated.

Andrei shifted and cleared his throat. "If the phone is on, the person wants you to be able to find it. We know better than to be tracked."

WE! Grimacing, Tori said politely, "Thank you for letting us know." She tried to keep the sarcasm out of her voice, but it was time for him to go.

Taking the hint, Andrei asked if he could speak to her for a moment.

Tori told Leslie and Renee that she would be right back. "Don't sneak out without me," she said, only half joking. Those two still had a ton of explaining to do.

When the door closed, they faced each other, neither knowing what to say. Andrei took the chain off his neck and handed it to her. "I want you to have this."

"I couldn't," Tori protested, offering it back to him.

"No, dorogoy." he refused. "You keep it. It's Saint Anthony. Maybe it'll do you some good."

Tori didn't want to argue. "Thank you."

"I hope to see you again…" he quirked his lips in a smile, "…under different circumstances."

"I can think of a few parts I could do without," she said wryly.

They stood in silence for a moment before Tori pressed the elevator button. Nodding, he walked on, leaving her life as abruptly as he'd entered it.

Tori stood in the hallway, momentarily staring at the necklace in her hand before slipping it into her pocket. Turning, she heard the sound of feet scurrying away from the door. She returned to the apartment, finding Leslie and Renee sitting on the couch.

"Sooooo…" Renee said. "What was that?"

Tori ignored her. "Leslie, I need answers from you right fucking now!"

Chapter 11

Friends Like These

T ori took a deep breath. "You left me. I didn't want to go into the club in the first place. Renee, I'm not upset with you. You met me yesterday, but..." she turned to Leslie, "...you believed a random guy when they said I deserted you even though I SPECIFICALLY said I was going to the bathroom?! What type of fuckery is that? And of all people, you lose the only Black girl in a Russian nightclub! HOWWWW?!?" Tori tried to reign in her screeching, but the shock of the experience had brought unspent fury out of her.

Leslie stammered. "I swear we didn't! We thought you were standing outside to get air because we didn't see your coat. Once they tried to push us inside the car, and we had to fight them off, we got really scared." Leslie looked toward Renee for support.

Somehow that made Tori angrier.

"If this were you, I would have called the fucking national guard. Shit, I damn near started a riot to find you in that club before I passed out!" Tori retorted angrily.

"Babe, I didn't sleep all night. I called and messaged you nonstop. The man answered your phone and said that he would meet us. We figured it was best to wait. We were so worried, but we hoped you would meet us here. If you hadn't shown up by the time we got the phone, we would call the police." Leslie's blotchy tear-stained face added credence to her story, but Tori didn't care.

Aaliyah was going to have a field day with this.

Oh, fuck! Aaliyah! I have to let her know I'm OK. Tori thought. *She probably saw my text and freaked out when she couldn't reach me.*

Realistically, she knew that the police wouldn't have done anything. There was a good chance that once the police found out she was Black, they would have dragged their feet even more. The safety of Black women had never been a priority. It happened all the time.

Since she had moved to the city, Tori had her apartment broken into, narrowly escaped a mugging, and had to fight off an older man who tried to grab her while she ran through the park. Each time, the cops told her that there was nothing they could do. They would have immediately believed she had run off.

"Listen, if we go somewhere together, we leave that place together. Nobody ventures off, and no one goes to the bathroom alone. From now on, we are attached at the hip. If one of us has to pee, we all have to pee. Got it?" Tori sighed; yelling was pointless.

"This has been one of the longest fucking weekends of my life, and it's only Sunday. We could've died!" Tori pointed out. "I don't think y'all have grasped how lucky we are yet."

"You're right, but you've heard our side. We haven't forgotten what we just saw. How did you end up with him?" countered Renee.

Tori scratched her neck. "Well, he took care of me last night."

Leslie raised her eyebrow and scanned her slowly from head to toe. "How did he take care of you?" she said with a knowing smirk.

"You know, I think I need a shower." Tori turned, trying to escape to the bathroom.

Renee laughed. "Oh no, no, no! You're gonna stand here and tell us what happened with you and Tarzan?"

"I already told you most of it. I kept blacking out. At some point, I remember Andrei getting me into the cab," said Tori as she recounted what she could remember. "He got me a hotel room. You two were already gone by then."

Leslie raised an eyebrow. "OK, but why was he still with you this morning? Did you—"

Renee blurted out. "You had sex with him!"

Tori groaned and covered her face.

"Tell us everything! What happened?"-

"He was hot. Was it big?" Leslie asked gleefully.

"That's what you're worried about?" Tori glared at her.

"You're the only one who got a happy ending out of this, soooo, yes?" Renee rolled over and nudged Leslie.

Tori hesitated, searching for the right words, "It was...complicated."

"What does that mean?" asked Leslie.

"A curved penis, I think." Renee laughed.

Tori rolled her eyes. "He may have saved my life, but he was also in on them almost selling us into sex slavery. Maybe it was an adrenaline thing...."

Leslie cut Renee off before she could ask anything else. "We have an hour and a half before we pick up your phone. Let's get ready, and then we can start figuring out what to do about Renee's things."

"Don't worry about my phone for now. I'm going to use my work line and re-route the calls. I want to get the original back. It has a lot of photos that I need," Renee answered.

"Oh, yeah," Leslie said, "Do you think Andrei's right? Should we try to pick it up?"

"I have no choice. I didn't tell you, but I'm more worried about what else was in the bag. I took my wedding ring off and put it in one of the pockets. I needed to see how I would feel without it, but I CANNOT lose that ring. If my husband comes to visit and he doesn't see it…." Renee trailed off miserably.

"We'll find it." It was unlikely, but Tori didn't want to add fuel to the fire.

She stood up. "Now, I have to go wash an attempted kidnapping and dick off me before we leave."

Tori walked into the bathroom, leaving Leslie and Renee alone.

"What if I lost it forever?" Renee asked anxiously.

"You're going to get it back. Maybe they turned your backpack in at the club. It's not like anyone would've even noticed the ring unless they dumped everything out," Leslie replied.

Renee wrapped her arms around herself tightly. "I hope they will," she said.

An hour later, the women were ready to meet the mystery man.

When they arrived at the meetup spot in Union Square, one of the guys from the party (whose name Tori couldn't place) stood near the train station entrance. As they approached, she watched him scan his surroundings with a hard edge in his eyes.

"No repeats. We're in and out this time," Tori cautiously reminded them.

"Ladies! Here's your phone. I even charged it," he said. Chuckling nervously, he shifted his body to face them.

Drugs? Tori wondered.

The situation didn't sit right with her, but she played it cool.

Taking the proffered phone, Tori thanked him. "I appreciate you bringing this back. We're missing more things, like my coat, bag, and phone. Is there any chance that you saw them?"

"I'll check with the boys. I called from your phone, so I have your number now," he said.

Fuck, time to change the number again.

Tori thanked him and signaled that it was time to leave. As the women turned to walk away, he called after them. "Hey, tell Andrei I brought your stuff back."

Tori spun around, but the man had disappeared into the crowd.

She had more questions than answers at this point.

Maybe Andrei figured it out and told him we were coming, she thought. *Even though we never said who had the phone when he was at the house.*

The logic could have been better. Tori opted to file this as something to figure out when alone.

Once they were safely away, Tori said she would call an Uber and go home. They hugged each other goodbye and hopped into their cars.

The adrenaline had worn off when she reached her door, and Tori realized how drained she felt. It wasn't like she had much sleep last night unless the black spots in her memory counted. Add on her encounter with Andrei...

Tori opened the door to the sound of the two cats meowing. "Hi, guys. I had a rough night, and I don't know if I want to relive it or pass out," she said, picking up Shadow and scratching Hank behind the ear.

The cats looked at her curiously. "Don't worry, I'll fill you in later," Tori said. She took turns kissing them on the nose as she filled the tub.

The water was "boiling a lobster" hot as she stepped in. Absently, Tori lathered her washcloth and scrubbed her skin until it felt raw. Her falling tears ran hotter than the tub water as she replayed her time with Andrei.

Chapter 12

Lima

She reached for the sheet to cover herself, but Andrei stopped her. "No." Another command. He grasped her other hand, holding it firmly above her head.

"Don't move," Andrei ordered in a low voice. Tori opened her mouth to protest when he kissed her again. Holding her wrists securely in his hand, he worked his way down, expertly finding every one of her spots. Anger and confusion built inside her as her body responded to him even though she didn't want to.

His sudden stop brought her back to reality. Peeking out from under the pillow, she watched Andrei's movements as he slipped off his pants and pulled a condom out of his pocket. Safe sex with a stranger. An oxymoron.

Eh...amendment...safe-ish. Tori watched him tear the package open with his teeth and put it on while he guided his way inside her. Andrei leaned to kiss her again, pinning her knees against her chest. The moment he let go of her hand, Tori grabbed him by the throat, taking Andrei by surprise. He grinned as she squeezed his neck, confident that her hands could do no damage even as his face reddened. The faces of everyone who had taken her silence for acceptance flashed before her eyes.

Not like this, Tori thought. Using her knees, she pushed him off and scooted away.

"You're strong," Andrei said, sitting back.

The sound of an incoming text snapped her back to reality. The bath water had turned cold. How long had she been in the tub this time?

She checked the phone. Leslie again. Tori turned the ringer off with a sigh. More to unpack with a therapist one day. She just wanted to crawl into her bed and pretend nothing had happened.

"You know what? I'm gonna do exactly that," Tori announced to the cats. Shadow and Hank yawned at her and settled on one side of the bed. Pulling back the covers, Tori lay down. A moment later, she fell into a deep, dreamless sleep...until a trumpet rang. Shit! Tori's eyes flew open. *How long have I been asleep?*

Fucking alarm clock! The sound was obnoxious, but without it, Tori would hit snooze until she was an hour late. It was already time for work.

The prospect of a new week always appealed to her, but this was not one of those Mondays. "I should call out." Tori groaned, rolling out of bed.

"Maybe it was all a dream," Tori told herself. With a heavy sigh, she began to brush her teeth. Casting a bleary eye toward the mirror, she screamed at the sight of large purple bruises across her body.

She turned slowly in the mirror, inspecting them. It had been years since her body was marked up like that. "Thank you for saving me again, Lord." She prayed, digging through her makeup bag for the right shade to hide the weekend's activities.

She would have to wear something to cover the welts at work. The horror of the marks was a testament to Tori's narrow escape. The wildest part was she still didn't know who or what to report to the police. Was it worth it at this point? How in the hell was she going to explain this mess?

Chapter 13

King "Leer"

The Walker Art House took up two chic floors of an old converted warehouse in Red Hook. Tori worked obscene hours and barely made any money, but anything was better than hours of discovery with her divorce lawyer. Hopefully, her boss, Diane, hadn't made it in yet.

God must've been looking out this morning; no Diane in sight, and she managed to make it there with 20 minutes to spare. Chef's kiss!

Tori tiptoed through the office, trying to keep a low profile until she reached the kitchen and faced her first nemesis of the day, their ridiculously complicated coffee maker.

Ten thousand dollars on a coffee maker, but I haven't had a raise in two years.

It didn't matter that she hated coffee; today, it was a necessary evil. All the extra sleep yesterday hadn't done the trick.

She poured a cup, closing her eyes to enjoy the scent of freshly ground beans.

"Tori, I need to see you in my office," a voice with a high nasal whistle said in her ear.

"Fuck!" Tori bristled. Careful to keep a pleasant expression, she turned to face Roger Wezel, VP of Marketing (and Diane's much younger husband).

A rat in every sense of the word, Roger's reputation for playing dirty was well known in the office, but as the owner's son-in-law, nobody complained. Roger's watery blue eyes darted furtively across her body while he waited for her to speak.

She looked around at the otherwise empty kitchen. *Why does he always try to talk to me in his office?* Tori nodded curtly, following him into the closet-like space with an underlying scent of Creed and unwashed gym skin.

A wannabe photographer, Roger covered every inch of the space with photos of bleak landscapes between shots of him shaking hands with notable figures. It screamed insecure and overcompensating.

He sat back in the chair while Tori stood in the doorway, reluctant to go further into the room. Something about him was unsettling. The way Roger's wispy mustache over thin, brittle lips stood out against his pallid complexion gave him the appearance of someone who hadn't spent any time in the sun—a vampire.

An energy vampire, Tori clarified for herself. She watched silently as he brushed a greasy lock of hair out of his eyes. *Is he waiting for me to speak?* She wondered, refusing to give him the satisfaction.

"I want you to hear this song," he said as he turned up the music.

Seriously? She stifled the urge to roll her eyes. Roger kept trying to make her his "Black-spert."

Tori hated working with men like that, obsessed with everything Black, covetous. "I always wanted a Black girl, but I never got a chance to act on it," he'd said, trying to peek down her dress at their last company dinner. She wanted to avoid him after that, but Roger would come looking for her when his wife wasn't around. Diane didn't like him working with women.

"Have you heard of this singer?" he asked, beaming like a regular Columbus.

It was Beyoncé. Really? It took a lot of willpower not to roll her eyes. "Yes," she answered. *Fucking moron.*

"You wanted to speak with me?" she asked with a tight smile.

"Yes." Roger sighed. He sat back in his chair, staring a little too intently at her chest before throwing a pile of paper across the desk. "I need this done by the end of the week."

He can't expect me to pick that up! She raised an eyebrow, but a deep voice interrupted, "Tori, just the person I was looking for. Can you come to my office?"

It was Paris, the CFO and her favorite work husband of all time. She nodded and followed him, leaving Roger and the stack on his desk behind.

At 6 feet tall, with a low caesar, umber skin, the faintest hint of 5 o'clock shadow, and cheekbones that could cut glass, Paris Stewart was one of the most beautiful men she'd ever seen. Even Diane seemed to be in awe, blushing whenever he spoke.

She followed Paris into his office and closed the door. "Thanks for the save."

He laughed, "That's what I'm here for, baby girl. Now where the fuck were you? I tried to call you for a double date last night."

Tori groaned. "I had a hell of a weekend."

"Well, you missed out. Your almost-date has a big dick." He waggled his eyebrows at her.

"Paris!" she scolded with a glance toward the door. Roger's annoying ass was probably on the other side, trying to eavesdrop.

"Tori!" he laughed, unfazed by the idea of being overheard. "Tell me you at least dumped that loser."

"Well…" Tori sighed.

Paris rolled his eyes. "Oh no! You know that sexy man-child isn't for you."

"Wellllll…" she cleared her throat. "No, but it's over."

"Bitch, what? How?" He pointed the finger at her accusingly. "Tell me you didn't blow me off to cry and watch white people movies again. Diiiiick, ma'am."

"I fail to see the benefits of emotional constipation, but I didn't sit at home." Tori huffed.

"You went out without me? The audacity!" said Paris with a drawl.

"Pick one thing to be mad at, Paris." She rolled her eyes.

Paris narrowed his eyes. "Wait! Stand up for a second."

"Why? No!" she protested.

Paris gasped! "I know that look! You arched your back this weekend!"

"Shut up!" Tori hissed.

"Details or I'm setting you up on a blind date," he said smugly.

She tilted her head. "Weren't you going to do that anyway? I'll fill you in later. It's a long wild story, and your favorite is trying to pin some extra work my way."

Paris sucked his teeth. "What does he want you to do?"

"No clue. Probably planning to steal my ideas again," she said bitterly.

"Tori…" he sat on the edge of the desk, turning her chair his way, "…you're too smart for this place. You need a new job."

Tori laughed uncomfortably. "That's not in the cards right now, and you know why."

"You won't go through this divorce forever, babe. Are you planning for after?" he asked.

"One day at a time." Tori stood up and hugged him. "I've got to go. I think I have a conference call soon."

Paris squeezed her tightly. "Fill me in at lunch. My treat."

"Can't. Talking with the attorney today." Tori groaned.

"Le sigh, bitch. Fine, but don't take any bullshit between now and then," he reminded her.

"Mhmm…I'll do my best." Tori winked and let herself out of his office.

They had this argument often. Paris was a pushy pain in her ass, and Tori had no idea what she would've done if he hadn't come into her life. In the three years they'd worked together, Paris had literally picked her up from the floor at some of her lowest moments. Whenever Diane went on a rampage, they would sneak away at lunch to sip on sugary cocktails at the bar around the corner.

Paris was known in the office for being an absolute terror, but as the CFO, Tori had to spend a lot of time with him. "He's the type to KNOW what season your shoes came out and TELL you," the recruiter had whispered conspiratorially.

The woman hadn't lied, and Tori didn't disappoint. Paris watched her walk into the room, taking at a glance her black open-toe privé Louboutin's, tailored Badgley Mischka sheath dress and the single strand of pearls she never took off, even when she slept. A firm handshake and some verbal banter sealed the deal. Fast forward to now, and Tori wouldn't know what to do without him.

Walker Art House was the type of company that looked great on a resume. The CEO, Errol Walker, was her favorite kind of disengaged owner, only interested in the bottom line. He didn't care about the art he displayed in his galleries. Most of it was considered avant-garde (code for ugly and overpriced.) Errol's Chicklet-sized veneers and connections kept the green flowing in every direction except toward her, but it allowed her to be creative. Something that she missed. Despite Roger, Diane, and the sycophants that hung onto their every word, Tori was grateful to have gotten the job.

She returned to her desk and found Roger's papers in her seat, DUE FRIDAY, marked in red on a post-it. *This motherfucker.*

Tori sighed, moved the papers, and checked her emails. Nothing drastic; Errol was out of the office this week and would check in periodically on how things were going in his absence.

She typed out a quick update and pressed send before checking her personal messages.

Nothing but bills and emails from her attorney.

It was always money.

The job came with fantastic networking opportunities, but Tori would have to take out a loan to pay rent if the divorce wasn't over soon. That was probably not an option, considering Craig had ruined her credit, maxing out her cards and never paying the bills. Every two weeks, Tori would be lucky to have about 200 bucks left to last for the next pay period. That was only as long as her lawyer didn't need more money for something. She spent more money on cat food than she did on groceries.

Why are lawyers so expensive? This one billed Tori $ 500 an hour, but she did all the work. Tori couldn't stand the man, but he was the only one who would take her case. Her ex's reputation for rubbing elbows with the right people preceded him.

Her phone beeped. It was a group text from Leslie and Renee. "Hey! How's everyone feeling?" Leslie asked.

"Still can't remember much. Are you OK?" Renee sent a second later.

Tori started to text them back but changed her mind. She didn't have an answer to that question yet. For one thing, she was still reeling about what happened at the club.

Based on the blackouts, she was positive that they were drugged. In fact, Andrei was the first one to hand her a drink. Then there was everything that happened in the hotel…he had probably set her up in the first place.

Tori had broken every rule she ever had about men at this point, and she needed to go to the doctor asap.

"Shit!" Tori said under her breath, checking to see if there were any lunchtime appointments.

Damn! They're closed! She thought. *I can't wait till tomorrow.* Tori panicked.

Her phone beeped again.

It was Renee. "Hello! Are you OK? Getting worried. We didn't hear anything from you last night."

"She's going to bug me until I answer," she realized.

Her phone rang. Stepping into a supply closet for privacy, Tori answered, "Hello?"

"Hey! I figured it was better to call you so I could say this fast. Are you OK? We were getting worried about you," said Renee.

"I'm as OK as I can be for now. I've been going over everything in my head, and I think we were drugged," Tori answered.

"I've been thinking the same thing; it was the vodka they gave us," Renee said.

"I fucking knew it. Well, I'm going to urgent care after I get out of the office," said Tori.

"Do you want me to come with you?" Renee asked. "I've been thinking about just going to the address that my phone is at."

"Yeah. Andrei said it was OK, but I don't know. We went through enough. The more I think about everything, the less I trust the situation," Tori said.

"The one who had your phone texted me. His friends have my bag. I gave him my work number if your phone died before we found you. I'm going to ride up to Brooklyn anyway, so I can meet you there," Renee told her.

"Have you ever been to Brooklyn?" Tori asked.

"No..." she said, "...I was going to use a map."

"Well, I'm definitely not letting you go by yourself. I'll come with you. At least this time, we have 911 on speed dial. Meet me at 5," Tori said.

"Perfect!" Renee answered.

"I'll send you the address; gotta go. Bye!" Tori said as she hung up.

Putting her phone away, Tori stepped out only to walk directly into the last person she wanted to see, Diane.

A beautiful, miserable woman, Diane Walker-Wezel was a Devil Wears Prada-styled nepo-baby who terrorized the people who worked for her with no shame. "What were you doing in there, stealing?" she asked with a nasty smile.

Tori was not in the mood. "Of course not," she replied "...Besides, I wouldn't steal if I wanted something. I'd look you in the eye and take it."

Tori smiled sweetly and walked away, leaving Diane speechless.

Shit! I shouldn't have said that, Tori thought.

She would pay for that moment later, but it felt good to shut that bitch up. Tori was trying to toe the line until she found something else, but her lawyer had suggested that she wait to switch jobs until after the divorce. Her ex was already after her nonexistent assets, and if he was petty enough to ask for palimony, who knew what else he'd demand?

A hand placed her forgotten cup of coffee on the desk. "Drink this... you look like shit."

"It was a shitty weekend." Tori groaned.

Paris looked around and lowered his voice. "Is it the ex? Don't let this suit fool you; I would beat his ass if necessary."

Tori laughed. "As much as I would love to see that, it's not about him. Leslie and I went to a club, and we got roofied."

"That sounds like my old Saturday nights." He snickered.

"Hold up," Tori laughed. "You're always on some crazy shit, and it is way too early in the day for one of your old ho stories."

"It's never too early for Dick Tales, but you're stressed. Listen, whatever happened, are you OK? Do you need anything?" He searched her face for clues.

Tori replied, "I'm fine. I think. There was this guy and…."

"A maaaaan! Well, why didn't you say so?!" he perked up. "That's why your ass didn't text me back. Did you stop pretending to be a good girl and take some new dick out for a spin? Bitch, tell me everythingggg!"

"Can you keep your voice down?" Tori scolded. "The last thing Diane needs is to know that somebody around here gets laid."

"Diane tried to prop up those wrinkled titties in my face the other day, still hasn't realized she's barking up the wrong tree." He laughed.

Unbeknownst to anyone they worked with, Paris was in the most adorably happy relationship possible. True couple goals! His partner, Marco, was a gorgeous chef with the body of a personal trainer. Paris swore up and down that he was not built for love, but one day they locked eyes while lifting weights at the gym. Technically, Marco was lifting weights, and Paris was scoping the scene out for any hot newcomers. It was love at first deadlift.

I should go to the gym more, Tori thought. *You know what? Never mind. I don't need to meet anyone. I think I need to be good after these latest shenanigans.*

"Hello! Hello!" Paris snapped his fingers. "Earth to Tori. Did you go down dick memory lane without bringing me with you? What happened this weekend? I want to hear all the juicy details."

"You're not going to leave me alone about this, are you?" She shook

86

her head. "Fine. Long story short, I went out with Leslie and one of her friends the other night, met a guy, got roofied, our stuff was stolen, he saved my life from some traffickers while also setting me up, and we hooked up. It was a lot. I really can't...." Tori said quickly.

"You can't do what?" Tori heard Diane's voice. "Be competent? Some people can't do their jobs properly. Right, Paris?"
   He bristled at Diane's words.

"No. Is that something you can relate to?" Tori mockingly replied.

Paris coughed, trying to cover up his laughter.

Diane opened her mouth to say something awful when Lana, the receptionist, interrupted, "Excuse me, Diane. Your husband is asking for you."

Diane snapped to attention and walked away, calling over her shoulder, "Find out when the campaign will be ready, Tori. I don't want to talk to you about this again."

"You didn't talk to me about it in the first place," Tori answered under her breath.

Paris let out the laughter that he had been holding back. "What was that? You never check her. If it weren't for you, I would've told that bitch about herself ages ago, and then I wouldn't be able to afford the engagement ring I'm thinking of..." he trailed off expectantly.

"Paris, you're already wealthy, and we both know they're never firing you." Tori's eyes widened. "Wait, you decided! When? Can I help plan?

87

FYI I'm wearing a tuxedo."

"Yes. On his birthday. Of course! You already know that my Best Woman better be the best-dressed bitch in there. After me, of course," Paris answered. "I've gotta move money around for Errol, but you and I will finish this conversation later. Drinks after work?"

"No, I can't. I'm meeting up with the one who lost her bag this weekend. I'm backing her up to go get it," said Tori.

"A friend!?!" Paris exclaimed. "Heifer, you aren't allowed to have any new friends. I'll let you slide this time." He winked and walked away. Paris was always a sunspot in her day, but even his presence couldn't shake the fear lingering in her mind. "Please, Lord, let me be fine and paranoid."

Andrei had worn a condom but even then...STDs and pregnancy.

Oh, Fuck Me! Tori started hyperventilating. Trying to breathe through a panic attack, she hurried to the blessedly empty secret bathroom and called Aaliyah.

"Hey, Ho," Aaliyah answered, blasting Soca in the background. The loud music surprised her. Aaliyah was almost always at work or in class during the day.

"Ho isn't the half of it." Tori groaned.

"Oh shit, what'd you do? I saw that text message you sent me. I was going to catch a flight and show up at your house until I saw Leslie post a video of you yesterday."

"She did? I didn't see it. Listen, I had a wild-ass weekend…." Tori quickly recapped everything that had happened.

"Damn, bitch. See…shit like this never happens when you're with me." Aaliyah scolded her.

"Mhmm— how many times have I been in a fight you started?" Tori joked.

"I'm retired now. Don't judge me." Aaliyah laughed.

"Yeah, yeah. I fucked up," said Tori.

"Good vibes, boo. You are fine. You're going to go to the doctor as a precaution. Don't start going into panic mode. Just be careful and stop hanging around with that girl! She's careless." scolded Aaliyah.

"I know you don't like her…." Tori started.

"It's not that I don't like her; I don't trust her," Aaliyah interrupted. "She left you. The other girl…whatever, but Leslie is supposed to be your friend. I would never leave you behind, and why didn't they call the cops?"

"I'm giving them the benefit of the doubt here because they are both covered with bruises. The guys roughed them up when they tried to snatch them, but, shoe on the other foot, I would've called the fucking cops," Tori admitted.

"Ex-fucking-actly!" said Aaliyah. "This is why I don't fuck with your friend."

"The feeling is mutual," Tori answered. The two had been like siblings for decades, but they gravitated toward different groups. It didn't matter, though; best friend time was sacred.

"Anyway…" Aaliyah changed the subject, "…I think you're fine. Just go get confirmation."

"I am. Renee is coming with me for moral support, but what if it's bad news? Remember, Craig did say I'd die if I left him. Can you hurry up and become a doctor already?" Tori said in a low voice.

"I'm working on it, and FUCK him. We've been through this a million times. The manipulative piece of shit said that to get in your head. He can't see the future. Everything bad he wished for you will go back to him." Aaliyah yelled into the phone.

Tori knew she meant it. Aaliyah had been her best friend since they were kids. Aaliyah was famous for getting Tori into trouble but was always right by Tori's side to help get her out of it.

"I miss you. You always know exactly what to say to me," said Tori. "I can do this."

"No, we can do this. You're not going to stress. I'm searching for an appointment now. Since your doctor isn't open and you'll lose your mind if you have to wait, urgent care it is," Aaliyah answered.

She quickly searched for the closest urgent care facility and made an appointment for Tori after work.

"Thank you, boo," Tori said, holding back more tears.

She turned off the music. "T— you might want to think about taking a Plan B."

Tori froze. "I don't need it. Once was enough."

"But−−" Aaliyah started.

Tori's phone beeped—a question mark from Leslie.

Shit... Tori thought.

"Sis, Leslie keeps trying to reach me, and Diane is on the warpath. I'll hit you later on," Tori told Aaliyah.

"OK, boo. Don't let that girl get you into any more bullshit, and bring that taser I gave you. Love you!" Aaliyah sighed and hung up.

Tori stared at the phone for a minute before responding to Leslie's message, "Hey! I'm at work. I'm going to stop by urgent care to get checked out, just in case. Renee told me she will be in Brooklyn later, so I will meet up with her. Hope you're OK."

She immediately got a text message saying, "Look at my arm." The picture attached showed black and blue hand-sized bruises all over Leslie's forearm and wrist.

Alarmed, Tori called her on FaceTime, "This is probably from the guys trying to pull you and Renee into the car."

"Jesus! I have the same marks all over my body," Tori said, peering down at the screen. "We need to take this as a sign of how bad things could've been. I've got mace, my taser, and 911 on speed dial. If you haven't heard from us by 7, call the cops."

She nodded in agreement. "Yes! Great idea. I think we all need to sit down after you two are done. Let's get dinner," said Leslie.

Laughing, Tori answered, "Oh, hell no. That's what got us in trouble last time. How about we meet at your place and cook something?"

"That's a way better idea." Leslie laughed. "Let me pick the menu."

"As long as it includes those cookies that you make. We'll call you when we're on our way back," Tori said.

"Sure. I'll have everything ready when you arrive. Let me know if you need anything. Love you!" Leslie said.

"I will. Love you too." Tori hung up and went back to her desk. She spent the next six hours distracting herself with work. Oddly enough, the rest of the day was smooth. Tori even got a head start on some tasks for the next day. Who knew an attempted kidnapping was all you needed to be super productive?

Around 5 o'clock, Renee called, "Hey, I'm downstairs. Ready to go?"

"I'll be down in a minute," said Tori. She grabbed her coat and made a beeline for the exit, narrowly avoiding Diane before she could demand overtime.

Chapter 14

You're Beautiful... Inside

R enee pulled her into a hug. "Did you make an appointment?" she asked.

"Yep. Urgent Care is only four blocks away. We can walk," Tori answered.

It was freezing outside, so they walked quickly, giving each other a run down of their day.

By the time Tori and Renee arrived, the place was empty, and they only waited 5 minutes before a nurse called Tori's name.

As she got up and walked toward the exam room. Tori looked back at Renee, "It's OK. You can come with me. I may need support. I hate needles."

After shutting the door behind them, the nurse introduced herself and began to ask screening questions. After entering Tori's basic information, she asked, "What brings you here today?"

Over the woman's shoulder, Tori saw the look of amusement cross Renee's face.

"I would like a pap smear and full panel STD screening," Tori started, trying to keep a straight face.

The nurse nodded without reacting.

Oh, I like this place. She's professional, Tori thought.

The nurse finished typing, took her blood, and handed Tori a gown. "Please put this on. The doctor will be with you shortly."

As soon as the door closed, Renee, sitting in the corner, said, "I thought you were going to tell her what happened on Saturday."

"Yeah...no. I don't think that she would've understood. She would probably want to report an attempted kidnapping." Tori sighed, looking at the bandaid on her arm. "When's the last time you got tested?"

"Before I got married. I've slipped up a few times since moving here, but I don't have any symptoms." Renee answered, flipping through a magazine someone had left on the counter.

Tori stared at her incredulously, "But... some people don't get symptoms before—"

A sharp rap on the door interrupted her comment and alerted them to the doctor's presence. This man had to be on the verge of retirement. The doctor looked like Mr. Magoo with tufts of white hair growing out of his ears, bifocals hanging off the tip of his nose, and shaky, liver-spot-covered hands. He introduced himself as Dr. Tempelton, giving Renee a once over, but a spark entered his rheumy eyes when he focused on Tori. As he looked down at her chart, Tori raised a skeptical eyebrow at Renee.

"Have you taken off your panties?" asked Dr. Tempelton.

Startled by the question, Tori sputtered, "Excuse me?"

She looked at Renee, wishing she could telepathically ask, "Did he just say that?"

Dr. Tempelton looked at her expectantly. "Did you take off all your clothes?"

Realizing he was serious, Tori stammered, "Uh…Yes. I am undressed under the gown."

The doctor smiled. "Lean back so I can look under the hood."

Tori's mouth dropped open, but she did as she was told, wanting to get this over with. As she placed her feet in the stirrups, the doctor reached under her gown, put his hand on her vagina, and squeezed it once.

"OOP-" Tori exclaimed.

"Bring it closer toward my face," the doctor said jovially.

Why does every word he says sound filthy? Tori wondered as she scooted further down the table. *I'm reading too much into this.*

A snort from the corner reminded Tori that Renee was still there. *I've set a new record. Three people have seen my vagina in less than three days.*

"You can stop there," said the doctor, patting her twice on the thigh.

"So, is this your girlfriend?" the doctor asked after a moment of silence.

"No. This is a friend of mine." Tori gritted her teeth and focused on the ceiling tiles.

This is some wild shit! she thought.

"So an STD panel and a pap smear, huh? Must've been a fun weekend." The doctor laughed.

Renee snorted again from the corner.

"I just want to make sure everything is fine." Tori sputtered, regretting the decision to make this appointment.

"Mhmm," the doctor said as he squeezed her left thigh. "Well, let's open you up."

Please stop talking, Tori thought as Renee's snickers increased.

The sound of a crank followed by a sharp pinch when the doctor inserted the speculum made Tori's eyebrows shoot up to her hairline, "Are we almost done here?" she asked.

"No. Barely started yet," the doctor said, "Doesn't look like anyone's been in here in a while."

"Oh shit!" Tori and Renee gasped in unison.

Before she could respond properly, the doctor removed the speculum and double-tapped her on the vagina again, "You're beautiful inside. I'll run the tests, but I don't think you have anything to worry about. You can get dressed now."

He winked and left the room.

As soon as the door closed, Renee let out a loud hoot, "Holy Shit!. He was hitting on you while looking inside your vagina. I've never seen a man smile that wide."

"Renee, I want to get out of here, get your shit, and meet with Leslie. Let's never talk about what just happened," Tori said, hastily throwing on her clothes.

Renee cracked a smile once they made it outside. "At least he said everything looks good."

Tori winced. "No, he said I'm beautiful on the inside. He could've been my grandfather. You can't make this type of shit up."

"Should we get tested to see if we were drugged?" she asked, turning back toward the door.

"I'd rather not go back," Tori said softly. The thought of facing that doctor again turned her stomach.

"You're going to be fine. Don't worry about it." Renee gave her a sympathetic hug.

Sighing, Tori asked, "So, what train do we have to catch?"

"Google says the Q train. The address is in a neighborhood called Sheepshead Bay," Renee answered.

"Why am I not surprised? I used to live over there. I know the area well," said Tori.

The women walked to the train station and waited on the platform.

"Have you spoken to Andrei?" Renee asked.

"No. I have too many questions that I'm not ready to get the answers to right now," Tori answered honestly.

"Well, I've been texting the one who has my bag. Thank God I still have my work phone, or else I would've been in serious trouble this weekend," said Renee.

"Yeah. I've been writing down and memorizing numbers all day," Tori said. "What stop are we getting off at?"

Renee checked the map, "It says Gravesend Neck Road."

"Oh! I used to live around the corner. I haven't been over there in ages," Tori answered.

Tori had lived there for a few years before she got married. Despite the turbulence in their relationship then, she had some beautiful memories of the quiet streets and walking to the beach to enjoy the sunrise alone. Tori cherished those moments. When they first moved to the area, Tori would encourage Craig to join her, but as time passed, she was always secretly relieved when he said no.

When they got to the station, Renee called the guy she was communicating with.

Within a minute, he pulled up in a black Escalade with three other men. Imagine Tori's surprise when she saw that it was Ivan, the one who tried to convince her that Leslie and Renee had left.

He walked up to them with a big smile. "My beauties!" he exclaimed. "You two are a lot of fun. No hard feelings, right."

Disgusted but not wanting to let it show, Tori answered, "Hi, Ivan. No harm, no foul."

"Good. You can tell Andrei that I've given you your things back," Ivan said.

My things? Andrei again? What The Fuck? Tori thought as the car door opened. A man she didn't remember meeting held out her coat and Renee's backpack.

"Oh, my God! I thought I would never see that again. Thank you for returning it," Tori said as she grabbed her coat, checking the pockets.

Her money, ID, and credit card were still there. *How much clout did Andrei have if he could make this happen?*

Renee rummaged through her backpack and closed it. "Thank you. I know you didn't have my phone, but the app says it's not far from here. Do you recognize this address?" Renee asked as she showed him the last known location of the phone.

"Well, I don't have it, but if the phone is on, whoever it is, must want you to find it," Ivan said with a laugh.

"Well..." Renee said as she turned toward Tori, "...it's only 10 minutes away. Can we drive by and look for it?"

Tori hoped they couldn't hear her teeth grinding in annoyance. The sooner they got out of this, the better. Adopting a cheerful tone, she said, "Sure. Let's get a cab now."

Renee ordered the car while Ivan fidgeted awkwardly in front of them.

"If you ever wanna party again, keep my number," said Ivan.

With as much diplomacy as she could manage, Tori smiled. "Thanks for the invitation. We'll let you know."

The cab chose that moment to arrive. After the car pulled off, Renee giggled. "Well, that was awkward."

"You think?" Tori answered, her voice dripping with sarcasm. "And now we're going to another random location to find your phone. It'd better be there."

"What if they don't wanna give it back?" Renee asked.

"Then you won't have a phone." She shrugged. One look at Renee's face showed that she was on the verge of crying.

Tori tried again with a sigh. "You can offer them a reward."

"What can I give them?" Renee asked, sending Tori a lascivious wink.

"Don't look at me!" Tori said, "I've already had thank-you sex for saving my life, so you know... the bar is set kind of high."

The two women cracked up while the Uber driver pretended not to eavesdrop.

They turned onto a quiet street of row houses a few minutes later.

Asking the driver to slow down, Tori asked, "Well, which one is it?"

Renee checked the Find My Phone, "It says 442."

They scanned the house numbers in the quickly diminishing daylight until they saw the right one. Tori asked the Uber driver to wait for a moment, telling him that she wanted to extend the ride back to the city.

The two walked to the house door, glancing at each other before ringing the bell. A moment later, the door opened, and a heavily pregnant Black woman stood with an annoyed expression.

"Can I help you?" the woman asked.

Confused, Renee glanced at Tori for help.

"Hi, my friend lost her cell phone at a nightclub this weekend, and according to this app, it says the phone is near here. Did you happen to find a…" Tori started, noticing that the woman seemed angrier with each word she spoke.

"Here?" the woman shouted. "Oh, hell no!"

Confused, Tori and Renee shared a look while the woman stepped back and screamed, "Clarence! Get your ass over here!"

A bewildered, tall Black man walked over to the door to see what the commotion was about.

"Visiting your Grandma, huh? Did you go to a fucking nightclub this weekend? You're cheating on me with these bitches?!?!" the woman screamed at the top of her lungs.

"Oh, shit!" Tori said. "Ummm, No, ma'am! We've never seen him before! She lost her phone at a Russian nightclub called Kremlin in the city. I can promise I was the only Black person there. I'm probably the only one that has ever been there. We've never seen this man before."

The screaming woman ignored Tori's words and wouldn't stop slapping him.

Trying to block the hits, poor Clarence shouted back, "I'm telling you, I didn't go to any damn nightclub. I've never seen this bitch in my life!"

Tori had just about had it with all the bitches they were throwing around. Still, to keep this woman out of early labor, she adopted the tone of a kindergarten teacher to diffuse the situation, "Miss...I promise we don't know him. I'm so sorry. We didn't mean to disturb you. We are looking for the phone. As I said, it was a Russian nightclub. He wasn't there."

Winded by her yelling, the woman shouted at Tori, "Well, clearly, we're not Russian. You have the wrong address. Go check with my neighbor next door."

Tori grabbed Renee's hand, saying, "You know what? Let's go. Thank you! We're so sorry."

They hurried down the stairs calling out as they ran to the house next door.

"Congratulations on the pregnancy! Sorry again for disturbing you!" Renee yelled over her shoulder.

Chapter 15

Crème de la Meow Meow

"Y ou know, we should've realized we were at the wrong place," Tori said.

"How would we know?" Renee asked, still looking over at the house they had just left where the angry pregnant woman glowered at them from the window.

The house next door had a giant Russian flag painted on the garage door.

"Lucky guess," Tori said dryly. "Listen, you knock while I tell the Uber to keep waiting."

Renee cautiously rang the bell while Tori stood on the stairs, motioning for the driver to wait. The door opened, and a man stood in the doorway.

"Hi, I lost my phone at…." Renee started, but before she could finish, the man interrupted her.

"You? You lost your phone?" he said.

"Yeah, on Saturday," Renee answered nervously.

Tori turned around to look at the person Renee was talking to when she heard him shout, "You!?!" and saw him point in her direction.

"It's good to see you," the man said with a big smile.

Confused, Tori looked around to see if he was talking to someone else.

The man flipped on the porch light and stepped outside. Something about him looked familiar.

"I'm sorry? Have we met before?" Tori said.

"You don't remember me?" he asked.

"Uh…No, but if you've found her phone, we can take it off your hands and let you enjoy your evening," Tori answered.

Renee looked back and forth between them in confusion, "Do you know each other?"

The man replied, "We met on Saturday. We need to talk."

Uncomfortable, Tori said, "You know what…our Uber is waiting for us, and we've got to…."

He interrupted her, "I will pay for you to get another Uber. If you don't remember me, you need to know what happened on Saturday."

Renee beamed. "She sure does." She ignored Tori's protests and called out to the driver. "Thank you! We're fine; you can go!"

Shocked, Tori called out, "WAIT!" but the driver peeled off.

The man held his front door open for the two to walk inside.

Renee glanced over her shoulder at Tori before stepping into the foyer.

"Not again!" Tori groaned. "Out of the frying pan, into the fire."

Holding on to the mace in her pocket, Tori watched the man close the door behind them.

Tori did a double take as she saw his face. What the hell? *Was there a sale on fine-ass white men that she didn't know about?*

Tori looked over at Renee, who was also gawking at the guy as he handed her the missing phone.

"Can I get you something to drink?" he asked.

"Uh, No. Thank you." Tori answered.

"I'll take some water," said Renee, a huge grin spreading across her face.

The man grabbed a bottle from a case of water on the floor and handed it to her.

An awkward pause followed, consisting of him staring at Tori, Tori checking for possible exits, and Renee glancing between them, amused by what was happening.

Impatient, Tori asked, "So…What did you want to tell me?"

"Well, you were pretty messed up, and you refused to go in the ambulance," the man said.

"Ambulance?!" Tori half-shouted. This was getting weirder by the minute.

"Wow. You don't remember me?" He rubbed his neck sheepishly.

"What's your name?" she asked.

"I'm telling this all wrong. Sorry, let me introduce myself. I'm Derek. I was at the club on Saturday. I saw you dancing with your friends inside, and then after the party was over, I jumped in the middle of the fight," he said.

"The fight?" Tori exclaimed. "I was fighting?"

"Kind of. I jumped in," said Derek. "I was there with friends, and as we walked out, these big fuckers were trying to put you in a car, but you were struggling. Something didn't look right, so my friend and I intervened. We got into a scuffle with them and called 911, but you refused to leave with the ambulance."

Her eyes went wide as the memories began to flood back.

After the bouncers walked away, Tori fell in slow motion and slammed face-first into the pavement. She was having trouble getting up when she felt herself being lifted again.

It was Ivan and a few other men from earlier. Roughly, they grabbed her arms and began to half carry/half drag her toward a black SUV.

She tried to tell him, "Just tell me where my friends are. I'll find them myself," but she was having difficulty concentrating. The only thing Tori knew was that she shouldn't get into that car. Tori's legs were dragging as she felt them pushing her into the seat when a deep voice said, "What's happening here? Is she OK?"

The men stopped their attempt, and Ivan said, "She's with us."

The man that Tori now knew as Derek said, "Maybe, but she needs to get checked out. You can't leave with her."

Sounds of a scuffle broke out as the shrill sound of an ambulance approached.

Tori snapped out of her memories.

What the fuck was that?

"Thank you for helping me, but I still don't understand. How did you wind up with her phone?" she asked.

"Well, I thought it was your phone. The girl I was with saw you drop it when you fell and hit your head outside. I took it from her and kept it on so I could give it to you personally," Derek answered.

"So your girlfriend was going to steal my phone?" Tori asked with narrowed eyes.

Derek blushed. "She's not my girlfriend. She's pretty upset because I didn't let her keep it."

Something small, pink, and fast scurried past their feet at that moment. Tori and Renee jumped in fear as Derek laughed at their reactions. "Don't worry. It's my cat."

He tapped his chest twice, and a scraggly Sphynx jumped on his shoulder. Tori and Renee shared a look while they suppressed their giggles.

My life is a fucked up fairy tale, Tori lamented in her head.

Derek continued his story. "You refused to get in the ambulance, but another guy walked over. He wasn't with the ones who tried to put you in the car, and you seemed to recognize him, so I'll let you go with him. I'm glad you're OK."

"Wow. So you saved my life too." Tori smiled.

"I guess you could say that," he stammered.

With a sly glance at Renee, Tori thought about what she had said in the car. "Well, how can I ever thank you?"

Renee coughed, spitting water out in the process.

Confused, Derek looked between the both of them. "No, I don't need any reward. I'm just really happy to know that you're fine."

Slightly disappointed, Tori nodded. "Seriously, I'm very grateful. Anything could've happened, and it means a lot that there are good people in this world."

"We should probably head out," said Renee, breaking the eye contact between Tori and Derek.

Derek said, "I want to pay for your Uber."

"That's OK. We're headed back to Manhattan," said Renee.

"Don't worry about it. Let me take care of it." He reached into his pocket, pulled out some cash, and passed it to Renee.

Chivalry is clearly not dead, Tori thought.

When the Uber driver pulled up, Tori reached her hand out to shake his. Derek pulled her into a tight embrace, ignoring her hand.

"Can you let me know when you get home safely?" Derek asked.

Touched, Tori agreed and entered her number into his phone. She waved goodbye as the car drove off.

Before she could say anything, Renee imitated Tori's voice. "How can I thank you?"

They burst into laughter. "You know I might've spoken too soon.

Maybe thank you pussy doesn't count."

The driver looked at them curiously in the rearview mirror before turning up the radio.

"This situation is getting crazier by the day. What are the chances of me getting saved by two of the best-looking men I've met in real life?" Tori asked.

"I don't know, but either one could save my life anytime." Renee cackled. She texted Leslie, letting her know they were on the way.

Traffic was clear, so it only took 45 minutes to get to Leslie's house. Once inside, they quickly recounted everything that had happened.

"Tori, you have to call him!" Leslie squealed.

"No. He saw me at my worst," said Tori.

"Babe, he kept the phone to make sure he got it back to you. He didn't have to do that; he sounds like a sweetheart. You should send him a gift card or something," Leslie said.

"I'll think about it. While he was talking, I started remembering more. Can we not talk about what happened this weekend? I'm still stressed out." Tori groaned.

"You're right. Hey, I'm considering having a party at the house this weekend. It would be best if you invited him and his friend. It would be a nice gesture, considering how they helped you." Leslie smiled sweetly, the wheels in her head already turning on how to play matchmaker.

Tori said, "I'll text him tomorrow."

"Wait until you see him, Lez!" Renee interjected. "He could call me anytime he wants. We could do a lot worse."

"Don't wait!" Leslie said. "Text him now while the moment is fresh. You promised to let him know you made it home."

"You're right," Tori said. "In other news, at least Renee got her stuff back."

"The phone is a bonus. It was the wedding ring inside the bag that had me panicking. It doesn't even seem like they went through the bag. With everything going on, I didn't get a chance to tell you that my husband called this morning. He's flying here for a visit," said Renee.

"When? What will you do?" Leslie asked.

Renee shook her head. "There's nothing I can do. He had already booked the flight. I will tell him that I want a divorce when he gets here. Even though we don't have a great relationship, I want to give him the respect of saying it to his face."

"That's the honorable thing to do," said Tori.

Renee nodded hopefully.

Tori's phone beeped with a message from Derek saying he would love to go to the party and wanted to bring a friend. With that out of the way, the three women spent the evening reviewing the guest list.

Chapter 16

A Party Ain't A Party

A few days later, Tori teetered on a ladder, hanging party streamers from the ceiling at Leslie's apartment.

"Can you pass me the tape?" she called out to Renee, who was a few feet away organizing a tray of hors d'oeuvres.

"Sure," Renee said, walking over with the tape. "Lez, can you check the food?"

Leslie walked out of the back bedroom with her purse in hand. "Everything is perfect. I have to run to the store, but I'll be right back," said Leslie, grabbing a cucumber sandwich.

"Damn!" Tori groaned. "Are we missing anything?"

"Just more plates. I may have invited a few more people," Leslie called out as she closed the front door.

"It's probably the people from the party she and I went to last night. Here, try this first," Renee said as she handed Tori a sandwich. "Are you excited? You said Derek's bringing a friend. What does he look like?"

Tori laughed. "Didn't ask. I hope this wasn't a bad idea."

Renee rolled her eyes and took a bite out of her sandwich.

"Derek was nice. I want to pay him back for the Uber. I feel guilty," Tori said.

Renee shook her head. "Don't make it a big deal."

"I don't feel right about taking his money. We don't know him!" said Tori.

"Tori! Never reimburse a man. I plan on getting to know him very well after tonight," said Renee with an exaggerated wink.

Tori raised an eyebrow but said nothing. She wasn't vying for Derek's attention. After a nail-biting week of waiting for test results, she wanted to celebrate the good news that she was still in perfect health and forget about the ordeal. Renee seemed to have other plans.

From what Leslie shared, Renee dated like she was catching Pokémon ever since landing in New York. The space from her soon-to-be ex seemed all she needed to throw herself back out there. Tori hadn't been that brave at the beginning.

Renee stopped at the door and looked through the peephole. "I didn't wanna talk about it with her here, but did Leslie tell you what happened last night?"

"Yeah. You two went out with some other friends last night, and you just said they're coming by tonight. Why?" Tori said, hopping off the ladder.

Renee lowered her voice. "She had a nosebleed at the club."

"Oh shit. What happened?" Tori asked.

"She went to the bathroom with…." Renee stopped talking as the door opened.

Leslie was back.

She ran toward Tori, thrusting a bag in her arms. "Here. Open this."

Distracted, Tori opened the bag and found a beautiful black silk dress she had been eyeballing from a nearby store. The boutique had gorgeous clothes but never had her size in stock.

Surprised, Tori hugged Leslie. "Wow! Thank you. You didn't have to do this."

"Not another word. I know you were thinking about buying it, and when I popped in, they had your size. Treat it like my thank you for making the house look amazing." Leslie smiled.

"What did you get for me?" Renee asked expectantly, grabbing the now empty bag from Tori's hands.

"Oh!" Leslie said, biting her lip sheepishly. "Um…I only got the dress and some more plates. I'll treat you to breakfast in the morning."

Renee narrowed her eyes and turned back to the food.

The doorbell rang, breaking the awkward moment, and everyone jumped into action.

"Our first guests! Go change, and I'll let them in," said Leslie as she opened the front door.

Tori hurried into the bedroom, dressed, and touched up her makeup. She was nervous. Even though they were in a controlled environment, she was slightly afraid of being at a party. This was the wrong time to have a panic attack.

Luckily, Tori had learned how to self-modulate over the years. She leaned against the wall, appreciating the pressure against her back. It was comforting. Ironic that having her back against the wall made Tori feel safer.

"Nothing's going to happen, woman," she said aloud.

Closing her eyes, Tori prayed. "Lord, keep me grounded and safe. Let this be a good night."

A soft tap at the door alerted her to someone's presence.

"Need any help?" Leslie asked.

Stepping away from the wall, Tori plastered a smile on her face. "I'm good. Just finishing up."

"Tori, you can't fix a masterpiece." Leslie gave her a look of approval before walking back to the door.

Tori laughed. "Takes one to know one."

"Come out!" Leslie sang as she left the room.

Taking a deep breath, Tori gathered her afro into a stylish bun, enjoying one last moment alone before stepping into the party.

About 30 people had shown up when Tori came out of the bedroom. It was an eclectic group. She was happy to see a few familiar faces had found comfortable perches to observe newbies and catch up with each other.

Renee walked over, handing her a drink. "He's not here yet."

Tori played dumb. "Who?"

Renee pursed her lips and looked away.

Something is off with her tonight, Tori thought, deciding to wait until after the party to get to the bottom of things.

Just then, Paris walked into the loft with Marco, his fiancé-to-be. As they made their way toward her, Tori decided to cut the distance and met him halfway.

"I'm so happy you made it!" she exclaimed as Paris pulled her in for a hug.

"You know I'm always down for a party!" Paris clucked approvingly at her outfit. "Love the dress. I see the titties are out to play. Where's Mr. Hero?"

"Not you, too." Tori groaned.

"What?" Paris said innocently, batting obscenely long eyelashes at her.

Those damn things couldn't be real! Men have all the damn luck. She rolled her eyes, "You know exactly what I mean, Paris."

"Heifer, I'm trying to see if we can get you laid again," he laughed.

"So, is this one less or cuter than the other lover?" Marco said, jumping in.

"Y'all gossip too much," said Tori with a prim sniffle.

Leslie ran over, greeting Paris and Marco with a double kiss. "Darlings! Thank you for coming! Before you ask, Tori's guest isn't here yet. Can I get you a drink?"

Their shtick was starting to get annoying. Tori shook her head. "Why are y'all making it a big deal? He might not even come."

"The country comes out of her voice when she's nervous." Paris snickered. Before she could come up with a slick response, she saw Renee gesturing excitedly toward the door.

118

Chapter 17

Tall Drink of Water

D errick stood in the open doorway, scanning the room until he saw her.

He looked good tonight.

Broad shoulders and muscles under the clothes. Keep it together, girl, she thought.

An audible gasp and a low "Biiiiitch" from Paris let Tori know that her description of Derek did not disappoint. A hush fell over the room as partygoers noticed him. They parted, watching him curiously until he stood in front of her.

With a big smile, he lifted Tori in a hug. "You look amazing," he said, kissing her on the cheek. Blushing, Tori felt like someone had turned the heat on.

Thank God for Melanin, she thought as she watched her friends struggling to control their amusement. As Derek set her down, it wasn't lost on her that he slid her body very closely against him.

She tried not to giggle inappropriately. The sound of her crew's laughter broke their mutual gaze. Clearing her throat, she said, "Let me introduce you to my friends. Starting with Paris."

"Enchanté," Paris said, extending his beautifully manicured hand.

Derek smiled and shook it. "Nice to meet you. I like your shoes." He pointed down towards Paris's gorgeous Givenchy Chelsea boots.

Blushing, Paris swatted his arm. "Handsome and good taste. Tori, keep this one around."

He hooked Marco's arm, pulling him toward the bar before she could respond. Tori breezed forward as though she hadn't heard Paris, "...and you've already met Renee."

Renee stepped around her and gave Derek a tight hug. "It's good to see you again," she murmured.

Taken by surprise, Derek took a small step away. "You too," he answered politely, turning back to Tori.

Amused, Leslie skipped her turn and shook his hand. "I'm Leslie. Welcome, and thank you for helping Tori."

Derek smiled. "I'm glad I was there. Your place is—"

"Where's your friend?" interrupted Renee.

The three looked at her in surprise, with Tori and Leslie sharing a quick side glance. *What was her deal?*

Derek raised an eyebrow. "He's finishing a call outside."

Leslie hooked Renee by the elbow and gently steered her away. "I think we need to go check on something."

"We do?" said Renee, smiling at Derek.

"Yes! We do," Leslie grinned, dragging Renee away.

"Um, I apologize for my friends. They all think they're comedians." Tori laughed awkwardly.

"Don't apologize. I like people without a filter..." he smiled at someone behind her, "...Tori, this is Lev." Turning, she saw a slightly shorter man with a blonde crew cut and bright blue eyes.

She smiled as he took her hand. "It's nice to meet you officially. This one hasn't stopped talking about you since that night." Lev winked and elbowed Derek in the ribs. It was cute in a frat boy kind of way.

"Really?" she smiled.

Lev continued, "Yeah. It's not every day that he meets beautiful women. He's shy."

Tori leaned in conspiratorially. "I'm sure you can break him out of that habit. Let me get you something to drink." She walked toward the bar gesturing toward the alcohol like a game show host.

Tori smiled at them. "So, pick your poison. What would you like?"

"Anything you give me," Derek answered. His tone made her look up quickly. *Was he flirting?*

Tori smiled nervously as she mixed up their drinks.

Passing a glass to each man, Tori started, "So Lev, I hear you played a part in saving me from that little adventure last week."

"They were a tough crowd. Natasha was pissed," Lev answered.

"Who?" Tori asked, glancing at Derek. The expression on his face told her that Lev was sharing TMI.

Lev kept talking as though he hadn't noticed. "Yeah. His date. She said she met you in the bathroom."

It took a second for Tori to put two and two together. The creepy chick from the line!

"Blonde hair, blue eyes, very thin?" she asked, watching Derek's reaction.

At that moment, Leslie walked over. "Pardon the interruption, but I need to borrow Tori for a moment."

Tori smiled. "Go ahead and mingle. I'll see you in a little bit."

Derek nodded, looking slightly crestfallen. Tori resisted the urge to turn around as she walked away and see if he was watching.

"He's gorgeous. You look like you need to be rescued. I want to introduce you to a couple of the people that Renee and I met yesterday. They're snobs, but they love you already," Leslie whispered, leading Tori to one corner of the living room. Three eccentrically dressed people were inspecting Leslie's piano as they approached.

Before she could start the introductions, they heard the clatter of a falling tray. "I hope that wasn't my Grandmother's silver!" Leslie groaned. "Be the hostess for me?"

"Uh, no problem," Tori answered as Leslie hurried to check on the kitchen.

Turning toward the guests, she smiled. "Leslie will be back in a moment. I'm Tori."

A tall, ginger peered down at her over a pair of horn-rimmed glasses and stretched out a sweaty hand. "Cornelius. Are you the divorcee that almost got kidnapped? I'm obsessed!"

I'm going to strangle her. Tori fumed inside but smiled graciously. "I'll add that to my business card, but I'm sure that story has been exaggerated for dramatic effect."

A thin woman with wispy bangs took a step forward and gave her two quick air kisses. "Jessica. So you three didn't run into the mob?"

"Uh...that part is accurate," Tori thought of ways to change the subject.

"Leslie told me about you. Aren't you a concert pianist?"

Cornelius positively glowed with pride. "That's right. Lez said that she had a model S in her living room, and I had to see for myself."

The final guest, a reed-thin redhead, didn't wait for him to finish. She hugged Tori tightly, "I'm Bridget J—s!" in a sing-song voice.

Tori blinked in surprise as she slid out of the embrace. "Sometimes, I am too."

The three howled in laughter, "Oh, you are delightful. No, her name is truly Bridget J—s."

Before Tori could come up with an appropriate response, Leslie was back.

"Yes, they mentioned that you told them about what happened," Tori said sharply. Leslie frowned and winced, catching her meaning.

Noticing Renee waving to her from across the room, Tori excused herself, "I seem to be popular today. I'll catch up with you in a bit." She walked away, following Renee into one of the bedrooms.

"What happened?" Tori asked as Renee ushered her into one of the guest bedrooms and closed the door.

"So, I asked Derek if he was interested in either of us. It seems he wants you," said Renee with an eye-roll.

Tori stared at her in disbelief. "Why would you even ask him that?"

"I was helping you out because if he wasn't really into you, then you wouldn't be upset when I--" Tori listened in annoyance while Renee explained the merits of her actions.

Tori exhaled. "Do me a favor, don't ever do any silly shit like that again. If I wanted to talk to him, I would. I don't need interference." She walked around Renee, opened the door, and returned to the party.

What the fuck? she thought. *That's the most immature shit I've ever heard.*

Tori walked over to the bar and made herself a Vodka tonic trying to reign in her annoyance.

"So you like vodka?" she heard Derek's voice say.

Turning around, she laughed. "It tends to be my drink of choice." She smiled. "What's yours?"

"Hennessey," Derek answered as he leaned close to grab the bottle behind her.

Shocker. "Huh. I wouldn't have pegged you as a dark liquor type," said Tori.

Derek raised an eyebrow. "What did you think I was into?"

Tori leaned back and gave him a slow scan from head to toe. "Tequila," she said confidently.

"And why is that?" he asked.

Adopting a serious expression, Tori leaned in. "You look like you like to party."

Derek let out a loud laugh. "I do. Not quite as hard as you."

Tori winced. "Touché. In my defense, I'm pretty sure we were drugged."

He grabbed her hand. "I'm sorry that that happened to you."

"So am I, but I'm grateful you were there. I don't know what would've happened, and I don't want to think about it," Tori said.

"Well, Cheers! To forgetting it ever happened!" he said as he lifted his glass in a toast. He waited until Tori took her first sip to say, "We can find a new way to tell the kids we found love."

"Wait, what?" Tori sputtered.

Derek laughed. "Wow. OK, maybe not."

At that moment, his friend walked over with Renee. "The host said you're running out of ice and asked if we could all go to the store and carry back a few bags."

Tori looked at Renee in confusion. "We can't have it delivered?"

"No." She grabbed Tori's hand and winked. "It's a nice night. We might as well walk over."

Picking up on the hint, Tori sighed. "Fine. I'll grab my coat."

Walking toward the coat closet, she saw Paris and Marco arguing in the corner. Strange, they were probably bickering over something silly, like who had the better sense of style. Rolling her eyes, she grabbed a jacket and met Renee, Derek, and Lev at the elevator.

The air outside was cold and crisp as they walked toward the 7-Eleven. Renee linked arms with Lev and dragged him toward the store talking animatedly.

"Your friend has a lot of energy," said Derek with a chuckle.

"She does. I haven't known her long. Renee is new in town." Tori blushed.

"Are you from here? I've been waiting for days to find out how you ended up in that club," he asked, slowing down his pace.

"I'm from Jersey originally. I moved out here as a teenager and never looked back. I was only there because it was girls' night and they wanted to go. You?" Tori answered as she watched Renee whisper something in Lev's ear that made him turn red.

What was that girl up to? she wondered.

"Brooklyn born and bred." Derek flexed his chest to emphasize his well-cut physique. A chest like that deserved a medal.

"I shouldn't have asked. You have that distinctively heavy Sheepshead Bay accent," she said sarcastically.

"Oh yeah, Jersey girl?" he said, exaggerating his tone. "You ain't seen nothing yet."

Cringing, Tori laughed. "Yeah, you're going to have to work on that impression. Nice try, though."

"OK, well, I've got another question for you. Outside of almost getting kidnapped, what do you like to do for fun?" he asked, gently placing his hand on her lower back as he held open the door.

"Do you know, I'm still figuring that out. I've been so busy. I haven't had much time for late nights. I only get to go out when I see Leslie or Paris. We were catching up when I met Renee, and a couple of hours later…I met you." She shrugged.

"Oh wow, so you just met!" he said in surprise.

"Yeah." Tori laughed as she looked over at Renee.

Renee ran her hand across Lev's back while he tried to pay for the ice on the counter. Derek's poor friend looked miserable.

"Um…should we go save him?" Tori asked.

Derek looked over and snickered. "No. He's a big boy, and he'll be perfectly fine. I want to start planning our date."

Date?!? Tori wondered to herself. *Oh shit!*

Tori looked toward Renee for help but saw she was in the middle of her own entanglement.

She laughed nervously. "Seriously, I think we need to intervene."

Poor Lev seemed to have his hands full between 4 bags of ice and Renee trying to pull him in for a kiss.

What the hell was up with her? While Derek and Lev divided the bags between them, Tori pulled Renee to the side.

"What's going on with you tonight?" she asked hushedly.

"Nothing!" Renee exclaimed. She seemed jittery, like she had mainlined caffeine when the party started.

Tori frowned. "Are you sure? Cause you damn near ripped his clothes off inside of the store."

"Relax. You don't know what you're talking about. He's into me," Renee said, storming off.

Contrary to Renee's comment, Tori noticed Derek's friend was walking away at top speed with all the bags of ice.

"What happened?" she asked, looking past him as Renee raced to catch up with Lev.

"I wanted to talk to you." He grabbed her hand. "Let's take a walk."

They walked silently for a few minutes before Tori interrupted the quiet, "So, I know I've said this before, but I want to thank you for helping me out of that situation. It's nice to know that there are still good Samaritans around."

"Any time. You made me feel like a hero that night." He beamed.

Tori laughed. "I wanted to ask you something. Why didn't you drop the phone off at the club?"

He smiled sheepishly. "Well, I figured you'd try to track it, which meant there was a chance I'd see you again."

"Seriously?" she scoffed. "It wasn't even my phone."

"Yeah, I got lucky," Derrick replied as he reached for her other hand. He pulled her close. "You were the cutest blackout drunk person I've ever seen."

Tori sputtered. "Wh-!" but before she could get the word out, he stuck his tongue down her throat. White rom-com 101, kiss a woman mid-sentence. *She wondered if men knew kissing someone until their teeth clicked was not a turn-on.* Was she hard on him? Tori wasn't sure. Her relationship with consent had been muddled. As handsome as Derrick was, her experience as a damsel in distress with him once was enough—a cute guy with bad timing.

She pulled away. "This is nice, but we should start heading back. The girls are still a little paranoid after recent events."

Derek looked like someone had taken the wind out of his sail, but he flashed a boyish smile. "Of course. I don't want anyone to think I'm stealing you."

Chapter 18

Bridget J—s, Baby!

He pulled her in for another kiss as they exited the elevator, but Renee burst into the hallway. "Torrr-Oh!"

Tori and Derek sprung apart from each other guiltily. She was glad Renee showed up. He was cute, but his wandering hands were a bit much.

Tori fixed her dress. "Hey! Is everything OK?"

"Leslie wants you." Renee watched them for an uncomfortable moment before slamming the door.

Tori was getting tired of Renee's attitude.

As she reentered the party, Tori saw everything was in full swing. At least 60 more people had arrived while they were gone.

The crowd was split into the usual NY party cliques. Socialites and influencers posed for social media-worthy photos at the window, taking advantage of Leslie's skyline at night. The artistically inclined clung to the sides of the room, sneering at each other's taste in art. The foodies helped themselves to the sandwiches Renee had worked so hard on while the non-eaters crowded each other, making odd concoctions at the bar. The smell of torched rosemary and lime was heavy in the air while discarded cups and sticky pools of spilled bitters covered the kitchen island.

Tori looked around the room for Leslie, but Paris caught her around the waist, swinging a drink in hand.

"Good! You're back! Let me introduce you to someone. She'll be right back, Thor." Paris winked and whisked her away, introducing her to Jonathan and Melissa, a smartly dressed couple that looked vaguely familiar.

"I love meeting Paris's friends." Tori smiled, shaking their hands." You both look very familiar. Have we met before?"

"You might be seeing a lot of him soon," Paris said, knocking back the rest of his glass.

Tori raised an eyebrow. Was Paris already drunk?

"We have." Jonathan smiled. "I came by your office to talk with Errol."

"Oh!" Tori replied. Oh shit. Paris wasn't the type to invite someone messy to the party.

She didn't need anything extra about her life getting back to anyone at the office.

Jonathan continued, "When he approached me about buying the company...."

"He's selling?" Tori interrupted, looking to Paris for confirmation. When he nodded, Tori's mouth went dry. "Sorry to cut you off. That was unexpected information."

"Errol should be making the announcement soon. From what I hear, you've worked very closely with Diane. Paris called you the mastermind behind a few of the plans she pitched, like the collaboration with the Fashion Institute," he continued.

Tori was caught between accepting the praise and pressing for more details about the sale. It didn't matter; Paris was going to confess everything he knew. Besides, she was proud of how that program had turned out. Tori had worked until 4 am for months overseeing the project and rollout.

Of course, Diane took the credit when announcing to the rest of the team, but it didn't matter. The showcase garnered interest from a few major buyers.

In a rare moment, a tearful Diane hugged her. "I wouldn't have been able to do this without you." Tori was touched. As tenuously held together as her life was, the job had been a blessing in rebuilding her confidence. She had given up on so many dreams over the years that there was always fear in Tori's mind that she wasn't doing enough.

Within a week, collaboration requests had increased 62%, and Errol was all over the talk show circuit milking every bit of public interest. The Walker Art House was back in the headlines in a big way, but somehow the atmosphere in the office was even tenser. Tori had hoped that she could leverage her contribution into a raise, but Diane had delayed her review date for months. Now everything made sense.

On the surface, Tori kept it together and smiled. "I'm very proud of what we've done. Errol has built an amazing team."

"I'm launching a new series in the next couple of months, and I'll need some help getting it ready for the public. Paris talked you up so much that we should keep in touch." He reached into his pocket and handed her a business card.

"We must run to another engagement, but I'll tell my assistant to expect your call." At that, Jonathan and Melissa hugged Paris and left.

Tori looked at the closed door and turned back to Paris. "What in the world was that all about?"

"Sounds like that was an opportunity, Jefe," said Paris. "Don't get mad. I've been dropping hints that it's time for you to leave that bitch behind." He grabbed her elbow and steered her into a quiet corner.

"You already know my situation, and now I might be out of a job anyway." Tori tried not to let panic set in. This was a terrible setting to find out you would be unemployed soon. She looked around the room, eyes settling on the fully stocked bar. "I hope that's enough," she murmured.

Paris rolled his eyes. "Before you say anything, I didn't know all the details until recently, and this isn't going to be why you get drunk tonight. I've known Jonathan for a long time. If he says that he's telling his assistant to expect your call, he isn't kidding. Besides, what would you do if she fired you?"

"I don't know what I would do then either, but something is better than nothing, right? If I get something better, Craig's—" Tori started.

"Stop saying that shit to me. Every time you mention him, I get a headache," Paris said, pulling her into a big hug. "Listen, don't worry about it. We'll figure everything out later. Anyway, your new boyfriend is trying to get your attention."

"Boyfriend?" She looked over her shoulder. Derek walked toward her but got half-tackled by Renee on his way over. "Oh hell!"

"Did she just—" Paris started.

"Yep. You should have seen her with his friend." Tori shook her head. "She's lost her damn mind tonight."

Paris stirred his drink. "It's probably the cocaine she's been sniffing."

"She is not doing coke!" Tori scolded. "Wait! Is she?" Tori barely knew Renee, but drugs would explain the erratic behavior.

Paris pursed his lips. "Mhmm. Don't say I didn't tell you."

Tori only had a vague understanding of coke and zero desire to learn more. Her parents didn't hide the realities of its existence, but nobody she knew admitted to trying it until she was an adult. Wall Street executives, salespeople, doctors, and lawyers seemed to be the biggest users in her experience. They had the most money and generally kept neurotic jobs requiring their brains to fire at all cylinders. A few of Craig's college buddies had shared wild stories about full-blown coke and Adderall addictions before graduating high school because of wealthy absentee parents with their own habits. In comparison, her friends and their fumbling attempts at smoking weed were pretty innocent.

She rolled her eyes. "Speaking of doing things people aren't supposed to...did I see you arguing with Marco earlier?"

"It was nothing. A little disagreement about some light flirtation," said Paris with a wink.

"Honey, you've got to stop," she said thoughtfully. "We were just talking about rings. If you aren't ready, then...."

"I know. I know. I have to keep Marco on his toes." Paris laughed. "Besides, you and I have a date at Tiffany's next week. Help me pick out something he'll be proud of."

"He's the most low-key man ever. He doesn't want anything over the top." Tori laughed.

"Exactly. That's why I need you. My Best Woman is the only woman for the job." Paris pleaded, batting his eyelashes.

"You're the only person who would take a divorcee ring shopping. And Tiffany's? Just how rich ARE you? No...don't tell me. Buy me a Zebra."

Tori was only half joking. She knew Paris came from a wealthy family down south, but he never wanted to discuss them. He always said that the family he chose was the only family that mattered.

"Speaking of things, you can ride." Paris gave her a hip bump. "Two white men in a row. You may be establishing a pattern."

Tori rolled her eyes. "Don't worry. No white-savior-complex here. I love Black men, even the ones who've disappointed the hell out of me. I'm just keeping my options open. I hope he's not one of those guys who wants a permanent damsel in distress."

"Invite me if he makes it long enough for Christmas." Paris snickered, "I want to see your father's face when he shows up like Guess Who's Coming To Dinner."

Suddenly, music blasted through the speaker next to them.

Glancing over, Tori saw Bridget J—s tinkering with the sound system. She looked around the room for Leslie and Renee, but they were nowhere in sight.

"Shit! Hang on one sec…." Tori told Paris. "I have to tell her to turn that down."

Before she could reach Bridget J—s, Leslie appeared, "Hi! Excuse me. I don't want to upset the neighbors, so we must turn the music down."

"Fuck the neighbors!" Bridget J—s shouted, smacking Leslie's hand away and turning the music higher.

The girl was hammered. She drunkenly flailed her arms around, trying to pull poor Cornelius into her dancing. He attempted to pull her away, but Bridget J—s refused to budge. Leslie looked over to Tori for help.

In slow motion, Bridget J—s turned around Leslie's speaker and smashed it on the ground like a rockstar, bringing the whole party to a screeching halt.

"Oh, shit!" Tori exclaimed, a sentiment echoed in the crowd behind them.

Bridget J—s smiled drunkenly. "You told me to turn off the music."

"It's time for you to go." Tori looked around for Cornelius and Jessica. Where the hell did those two disappear to?

The other guests stared at the scene in shock, tittering with each other over the dramatic turn the night had taken.

"You can't throw me out, you bitch!" Bridget J—s sneered in Tori's face. Her breath reeked of tuna dip and tequila. Tori looked around for help, but Leslie was off searching for the other two, and Renee had cornered Lev behind the bar. She watched what was happening without taking a step over to help.

Once that hot breath hit her, Tori had enough. "Whew! Yep. Somebody come get her. NOW!"

A panicked Cornelius scurried out of one of the guest bedrooms clutching Bridget's coat while Jessica tried to coerce her out of the door.

"Lez, we're so sorry about this," he apologized. "Honey, let's put on your coat and get you out of here."

"I'm not going anywhere until this CUNT apologizes!" Bridget J—s shouted as she lunged out of Jessica's arms.

It took a moment for Tori to realize that Bridget J—s was glaring at her.

"Is she talking to me?!" she asked in surprise. "A cunt? Girl, Fuck you." Fed up, she turned to Cornelius. "I'm going to make this very clear, get your friend in line, or I'm calling the cops."

Bridget J—s' friends tried to corral her out the door, but the girl was determined to make a scene. She ran to the kitchen, swept over a few bottles, stuffed a sandwich in her pocket, and ran out of the front door.

Leslie looked like she was ready to cry. "Can you make sure that she's gone?"

"Do I look like security?" Tori asked. "You know what, never mind." This situation was going left very quickly. Under normal circumstances, Tori would have just gone home. Nothing good ever came from intervening in confrontations with young, drunk white women, but unfortunately for her, Bridget J—-s was blocking the only exit.

Walking into the hallway, Tori saw Bridget J—s's friends still trying to coax her into the elevator.

"I don't wanna take the 'vator!" She shouted, drunkenly pushing them

139

away. "I'm r-ride the stairs."

The girl couldn't even form a proper sentence, let alone walk down 20 flights. Concerned, Tori said, "This is the penthouse. For safety, I don't think--"

"Mind your fucking business." Bridget J—s screamed.

A crowd had formed in the doorway to Leslie's loft, and nosy party-goers had a first-hand view.

If Bridget J—s managed to place a finger on her, Tori was going to beat her ass. But if Tori did that, the likelihood of winding up in handcuffs for even thinking about an altercation with a white woman probably rose by 80%. Miss J—s may have hit the limit of Tori's patience, but she damn sure wasn't worth her freedom.

"You know what? This is NOT my business. Y'all be safe now!" she called out, opting to watch the foolishness. Tori had done more than her part.

"Bridget, honey, please let's go!" Jessica cajoled gently, holding Bridget by the elbow.

"I'm Bridget J—s!" She corrected Jessica. Bridget pulled her arm away and pushed open the stairwell door. "I'm taking the stairs! Party sucked anyway!"

In slow motion, they watched as Bridget tripped and tumbled down the stairs.

Screams of shock rang out, and everyone ran to the stairs to check on her, but Bridget J—s was undefeated.

"I'm OK!" She dusted herself, removed her shoes, and limped barefoot down the stairs.

Incredulous guests walked back into the house, laughing over what they had seen.

"What a psycho!" someone called out. A few cheers broke the tension.

Someone had cleaned up the mess while they were gone, and music was playing at a respectful level.

Seeing her come into the room, Derek rushed over, "Hey! That was wild. Can we talk for a second?"

"Sure," she said. Tori was relieved to escape the craziness, but an ear-splitting scream cut her break short.

From across the room, Tori watched in horror as Renee picked Lev up like a rag doll and threw him against the wall. Lev's mouth formed a perfect O as he realized what was happening. The poor man's head hit the wall with a thump.

Renee realized she had drawn the crowd's attention, turned quickly, and ran into the guest room.

Tori and Leslie ran after her while Derek rushed to Lev's side.

Inside, they found Renee sobbing on the bathroom floor.

"Did he hurt you? I'm calling the police!" Leslie reached in her pocket for her cell phone and poked her head out the bathroom door to turn people away.

"What just happened?" Tori asked as Renee rocked back and forth.

After a few moments, Renee hiccupped, "H-h-he called me fat!"

"What?!" Leslie and Tori exclaimed.

"Lev called me fat!" she screamed, pointing at the door. Someone turned the door handle, trying to come in. Leslie, who was closest, poked her head out, speaking quietly to whoever was on the other side while Tori tried consoling Renee.

"I can't believe he said that. We'll kick him out." Tori handed her some tissues. Nothing about this night made any sense.

Tori stood up, intending to ask them to leave, when Renee continued, "He flirted with me all night, but when Lev said they had to leave soon, I asked for his number. I thought he was into me, but then he said that I wasn't his type and that he had a girlfriend."

Confused, Tori glanced at Leslie, "But Renee...you have a husband."

Apparently, that was the wrong thing to say.

Renee began wailing while Leslie struggled to hold back her laughter.

Suddenly, the door opened, and Paris popped his head in with a cheerful, "Hey!"

"One sec--" said Leslie as Renee screamed, "Get out!"

He slammed the door quickly, and Leslie pulled Tori to the side. "I think it's time to end the party. I'll stay with her. Can you--"

Tori nodded. "You should tell everyone. I'll talk to Renee. Can you check on Lev? I hope he doesn't call the cops."

Leslie nodded and left.

Tori looked over at Renee, still sitting on the floor, hugging her knees, and sighed. They sat together, saying nothing for a while, the sounds of the party dwindling in the background.

Reaching into the cabinet, she grabbed a washcloth and wet it in the sink.

"Renee?" she asked, offering the wet towel. Noticing for the first time streaks of chunky black mascara staining her fingers, Renee took it, nodding her thanks.

After a few more minutes, Tori asked, "Sweetheart, what's happening? You've been upset all night." She hoped this counted as opting for a gentler approach.

Renee leaned against the wall. "He reminds me of my husband."

The door opened, but it was Leslie. "I cleared the house. How are you feeling, babe?" Leslie handed her a bottle of water before lowering her voice. "Did she tell you anything else?"

She cast a nervous glance toward Renee, afraid to set her off again.

Renee took a sip before apologizing. "I'm sorry that I ruined your party. I didn't mean for this to happen. He just upset me so much…."

Leslie cut her off, nodding in understanding. "Don't worry. The party was basically over. If it makes you feel any better, you weren't the most exciting portion of the evening. Anyhow, now we can talk about Bridget FUCKING J—s!"

Leslie, Tori, and Renee left the bathroom and sat on the bed.

"That nutcase is going to be sore in the morning." Leslie and Tori laughed.

"What are you talking about?" Renee asked.

"Didn't you see her spectacular tumble?" asked Leslie.

"No…" she started, but Leslie cut her off sharply. "You must've gone to the bathroom, Renee."

Tori raised an eyebrow. *Wasn't Renee in the room when the situation started?* She had assumed Renee watched the entire thing.

Renee appeared lost. "Oh. Um. Th-that's right. There was a line," she explained, looking to Leslie for confirmation.

Shrugging it off, Tori dramatically reenacted everything that Renee had missed.

Howling in laughter, she asked, "Wait, Bridget J—s was her real name?"

"I know. I said the same thing, but she showed a few people her license. We should've known the girl was nuts the moment she introduced herself. She only answered to her full name the entire night." Tori rolled her eyes.

"Damn! We didn't take any photos," Leslie realized. "Renee, fix that makeup, and let me get my phone."

Leslie walked out of the room. "I can't find it," she called. "Can you call me?"

"Already on it," Tori answered. She called the number, but no one heard the ringer. "That's weird. Did you put it on silent?"

"No, of course not, and there is no way it's dead. The phone was plugged into the speaker. That's how I controlled the music until she threw it," Leslie recalled. "It must be here somewhere."

"Track it just in case," said Tori, searching the bed as Leslie grabbed her laptop.

"Bloody hell!" Leslie exclaimed. "What's it doing uptown?"

"Somebody took your phone? We should call the police!" Renee started to dial 911, but Leslie stopped her.

"No. It must've been an accident. I'll keep calling. Someone will answer." Leslie's tone was cheerful, but the worry on her face betrayed her.

"A lot of people were drunk. You'll get it back. Somebody probably thought it belonged to them." Tori tried to sound hopeful. "Don't worry. If we could get my phone back from the mob, we can get yours back from one of your friends."

"Speaking of friends...." Renee leaned forward on the bed, "...what happened with Derek?"

"Nothing. He kissed me, but the entire situation seemed messy. Do you know he kept the phone so I could track it and see him again? That's crazy. It wasn't even mine!" Tori rambled, listing all the reasons Derek was a bad idea. "He could've just turned it in and left his number at a precinct or something."

"That place was pretty shady. He probably wasn't going to a police station." Leslie grabbed her digital camera and began snapping photos of the two of them.

"Fair enough, but I'm not sure I need to go any further with that adventure." Tori shook her head.

Renee smiled. "If you don't want him, can I have his number?"

Tori's jaw dropped, and Leslie stopped taking photos.

"Has anyone told you that you have a one-track mind?" Tori asked. It took a bold bitch to ask a question like that. *How low was Renee willing to go?* This was the first time she had run into this issue. None of her friends would even consider a man that showed interest in Tori first.

Renee swatted at Tori playfully. "...but I need a pick-me-up. The one I had sex with last night was lazy in––"

"How do you compartmentalize like that?" Tori asked incredulously.

"Tori, we should go have a drink." Leslie interrupted, trying to diffuse the tension.

"No." Tori brushed her off. "Renee, you cried about being rejected by Lev, who you just met tonight; you cried about your ex-husband, you asked for the number of a man you just saw kiss me, and now you want to tell me about some guy from last night? You're wild as hell for that."

Renee's eyes welled up with tears. "You don't understand! My ex called this morning and told me I've spent enough time out here, and he thinks it's time for us to have a baby."

"Listen, I get it. I really do," Tori interrupted. "But have you considered that you might be acting out because of the divorce?"

"I thought neither of you wanted kids," Leslie asked gently, placing a hand on Tori's arm.

"We didn't, but he's changed his mind since I've been gone. He wants me at home with the kids while he continues the family legacy. I would love that, but not with him." Renee dabbed at her eyes.

"But what does that have to do with what happened tonight? I still don't understand why you threw that man against the wall," Tori asked.

An ugly expression crossed Renee's face. "I don't understand why you're being a bitch about it." She pointed at Tori accusingly. "You argued with Bridget J—s, and now you're trying to pick on me?"

Tori tilted her head to the side. "Hold up! A bitch?!?! First of all, I'm not falling for your crocodile tears. Second, let's not pin any of Bridget J—s bullshit on me. I didn't say a word until after she smashed the speaker. As a matter of fact, weren't they YOUR friends? "

Renee sputtered. "I only know Cornelius and Jessica. I had never met Bridget J—s."

"Yet you didn't intervene or check on either of us?" Tori scoffed.

"I was busy," she said smugly.

"Busy doing what?" Tori asked.

They glared at each other until Renee broke eye contact.

"I've been through a lot today. I'm going to go home." She walked out of the room with Leslie trailing behind her. Tori sat on the bed, fuming. The sound of the front door closing alerted her to Renee's departure.

Leslie walked in sheepishly. "Don't hold it against her. She was drunk."

Tori scoffed. "That's no excuse. She threw a man, instigated drama, and cried to make us feel bad for her. That's called manipulation, Leslie. You know what else? Do me a favor; warn me first before you bring that girl around me."

"But she's not a bad person. She's just tired," Leslie explained. Her excuses were flimsy at best.

Tori cut her off. "Tired is one way of putting it. Leslie, she's feeding you bullshit. You didn't see her at the store. Renee basically molested Lev and then attacked him. He looked like he wanted to get away from her the entire night." Tori shook her head. Renee's story didn't add up, but Tori didn't have the energy to explain it anymore. "You know what, never mind. We should start cleaning up."

Leslie nodded her agreement, dropping the subject happily.

The two walked around the loft slowly, taking in the mess. Leslie walked to the other ensuite bathroom while Tori carefully swept broken glass from the bar into the dustpan. As Tori dumped the glass into the garbage, she heard a shout followed by "Oi! Fucking hell!"

Chapter 19

To Catch a Thief

L earning American profanity was one of Leslie's favorite pastimes, but slang from across the pond was reserved for only the most grievous offenses.

Leslie missed a flight once, and the berating that she gave the poor customer service rep made Tori take the phone away and finish the negotiations herself for fear of Leslie ending up on the No Fly list.

"You kiss your mother with that mouth?" Tori sashayed into the bathroom laughing but was unprepared for the sight that greeted her.

Vomit. Was. EVERYWHERE!!!!! Exorcist-style chunks had congealed on the walls. The culprit hadn't bothered to open the lid to the toilet!

It looked as though someone had hastily attempted to clean the floor (as evidenced by the balled-up bath towels covered in vomit), realized they were making the mess worse, and ran off.

"Oh, My God! Who did this?" Tori retched at the smell as Leslie pulled wads of tissue out of the drain.

Cleaning up is the worst part of parties.

No one ever respected your house as though it were their own, but experience had shown her that it happened more when white people were involved.

Keg culture, she figured.

The obsession with Project X-style parties that ended in injuries and arrests always baffled Tori.

You would be hard-pressed to find a Black person brave enough to destroy someone's house like that unless there was a fight. The thought alone of not cleaning up after herself called into question generations of home training and a culturally collective fear of having to buy something if you break it.

Couldn't be me, she thought.

Tori shook her head and turned to Leslie. "Who were all those people?" There had been a lot of unfamiliar faces in the crowd tonight. Tori had missed so much of the party playing peacekeeper that she barely met any other interesting guests.

"Well, Renee introduced me to Jessica and Cornelius at a bar last night, and I told a few people to bring their friends, but...." Leslie looked at the ceiling thoughtfully, "…I've never seen most of them."

She looked at Tori and shook her head. "I see where your mind was going. You stress too much. It was my house; nothing was going to happen. So let me tell you what you missed…."

Tori half-listened to Leslie's stories about the rest of the guest list. Shaking her head, she closed the garbage bag and stood up. "Look, it's your house. But we have got to do better 'cause self-preservation skills are not that great in this group. I'm almost positive some of them were on something, Renee included."

"Tori…" Leslie said patiently, "…if you don't invite strangers, you will never meet any new people."

It was a fair point that Tori had no rebuttal for. The best thing about living in New York was among its people. Was she looking for the boogeyman in every corner because life had given her a few knocks? Fear wasn't the way to move forward.

Tori sighed. "Just be careful and vet them next time. You heard her the other night. I don't trust her. Renee's the type to bring coke and plant it on someone. I'll be damned if I get caught in some mess because of her cause when the cops show up, and I'm the only Black person in the room, they're gonna think I'm the dealer."

Leslie started, "You're being paranoid. No one would make that assumption because you're Black."

Tori shook her head at Leslie's naivety. She loved her friend, but seeing that "they're always trying to make it a race thing," expression cross

Leslie's face grated on her nerves. Tori wasn't anti-white; she didn't want to get caught in more bullshit because her white friends got to walk around with selective blinders. Maybe expecting a wealthy Brit to understand where Tori was coming from was too much to ask. It's not like people were eager to acknowledge their part in weaponizing race on her side of the pond.

"I'm not. I once got arrested in a white neighborhood because cops didn't think I belonged in the area. I was literally outside of my own house. I don't get to walk through the world the way you do. " Tori stopped, not feeling up to giving Leslie a history lesson.

"Here…" Tori handed Leslie her phone, "…you should call again to see if someone picks up."

Luckily, someone answered.

"Hello!" Leslie said brightly. "You've found my phone. Can we meet so I can claim it?"

"Who are you?" a woman asked in a hushed tone. In the background, sounds of classical music came through the speaker.

Biting her lip, Leslie looked at Tori for help. "Well, you have my phone, and I'd like to get it back. Who is this?"

"Oh, this is your phone? It was an accident!" the woman answered.

Tori listened to the speaker, trying to place the voice. "Hi, who is this?" she asked, hoping the woman would identify herself.

"I'm Bridget J—s," the woman declared, raising her voice. "Yeah, uh… my uh…My friend accidentally picked up your phone. Um, I can… meet you tomorrow and give it back."

"OK, Bridget, where can I meet you?" Leslie asked, rolling her eyes.

"It's Bridget J—s," she repeated firmly. "Tomorrow at 7 pm. The coffee shop in Columbus Circle. I'll text this number when I'm there."

"Got it! Thank you!" Leslie said, but Bridget had already hung up the phone.

"Of all people! I think you hurt her feelings. Considering how she rolled out of here, it might've been an accident." Toni snickered.

"Can you spend the night since she has your number? Brunch is still on me," Leslie said, surveying the now-spotless bathroom.

Tori thought about the rest of the mess in the living room and yawned, "Fine, but we've done enough for the night. You can hire someone to finish. I'm going to bed. Night." She walked into one of the bedrooms and looked at her phone. *I should probably apologize to Derek and find out what happened with Lev.* She wasn't sure what to say, but maybe a decent night's sleep would put her in a better headspace.

The next morning, Renee was already sitting at the table when they arrived for brunch. Tori whispered to Leslie as they approached. "You should've told me she was still coming."

Renee and Leslie chattered happily as the mimosas flowed while Tori focused on her food. She had not eaten much the night before and

154

had little to contribute.

Renee, who began drinking before their arrival, was feeling loose by the time she started talking about Lev. Tori's ears perked up as Renee recounted their interaction at the store. Everything Renee said was completely different from what she'd seen with her own eyes.

"Lev was all over me until Derek got jealous and made him carry the bags home," Renee told Leslie. Turning to Tori, she asked if he'd called yet.

That was not how Tori remembered it. "No," Tori paused, "I plan on talking to him about what happened with Lev."

"Good. Just because he has a girlfriend doesn't mean he's hot enough to turn me down." Renee smiled drunkenly.

Leslie spoke before she could.

"But he called you fat?" Leslie asked, still looking at Tori in confusion.

"I mean, no, but that's what he meant. He only said he had a girlfriend because he thinks I'm too fat for him." Renee tilted back her glass, signaling the waiter for another pitcher, oblivious to the looks she was getting from across the table.

"So, you lied," Tori stated simply. She signaled the waiter for the check.

"I think I'm missing something. If he didn't say that, why did you attack him?" asked Leslie, hoping for a better explanation.

Renee laughed. "Why are you being so uptight? You're never going to see them again."

"Do you have the slightest clue how bad last night could have been because of you?" Tori shook her head. This was precisely the type of shit that she was afraid of.

Renee's bottom lip quivered on cue, and she began to cry. "He just--"

"Save it, Renee," Tori interrupted. "We made excuses for you and ended the party because we were concerned only for you to lie about Lev? For what? Attention? That's fucked up."

Tori stood up. "Leslie, didn't you have an appointment to make?"

As they walked out, Renee called out, "But we can order another pitcher--"

Once outside, she signaled a cab to take them back to Leslie's place. They sat in the back seat quietly, each lost in their thoughts until they were safely at the loft.

"Why do you think she did it?" Leslie asked, breaking her silence.

Tori bit back the words running through her mind.

More times than she could count, Tori saw people rush to the aid of a crying white woman only to find out the entire story was made up.

Tori rubbed her temples. "For your sake, I tried to keep an open mind, but I never want to see her again."

She held up a hand to stop Leslie's protests. "Before you say it, understand this; I couldn't care less about a man. This is about right and wrong. I don't get to walk around oblivious or unaffected because if Renee ever lied about me, the consequences would be worse than leaving a restaurant. She riled us up to defend her honor and then lied. That story ends with my face on a t-shirt and her crying on TV. I'll pass."

Leslie nodded. "I don't blame you. I don't think she meant any harm, but she was upset that things were going so well for you. I think it started when I bought you the dress."

Tori rolled her eyes. "I genuinely don't care."

"I feel awful about not checking on Lev," Leslie said sadly.

"So do I," Tori answered, checking her phone. A message from Bridget J—s popped up "It's her. She wants to meet at Starbucks on 72nd street in an hour." Tori read.

"Perfect. Let's head out now," Leslie answered, grabbing both coats.

Bridget J—s wasn't in the store when they arrived, so Tori grabbed a table while Leslie bought snacks.

"I still can't believe we all lost our phones," said Leslie as she crunched on chocolate-covered almonds she had bought while they waited.

"Technically, they were stolen." Tori laughed in disbelief. They were the luckiest women in New York. Even Renee's crazy ass managed to walk away from everything unscathed.

157

"Would it be wrong to ask how her friend ended up with my phone?" Leslie bit her bottom lip anxiously.

"It's a fair question. Here she comes." Tori watched as Bridget crossed the street nervously, scanning the window. A frightened look crossed her face as she recognized them. Entering, Bridget J—s walked across the room, dropped the phone on the table in front of them, and ran out of the door.

Leslie grabbed the phone, running after her to the surprise of startled onlookers.

"Bridget J—s!!" She called after the quickly fleeing thief. "Wait! We want to ask you a question."

"Ah shit," Tori muttered as she tried to catch up. Bridget J—s zigzagged, running through oncoming traffic to cross the street. *This bitch needs to be a running back with the legwork she was doing.*

"Why are you running?" Tori called after her.

"It was an accident!" Bridget J—s shouted, picking up speed. Leslie had almost caught up to her when a sharp twinge of pain in Tori's ankle reminded her how ridiculous this was.

"Dammit, Bridget J—s! Don't make me hop after you!" she yelled, slowing down.

With a quick turn, Bridget Jones shouted, "I'M SOOOOOR-RRRRYYYY!" she ran to a brownstone, hurried up the stairs, and slammed the door.

By the time Tori caught up, she was limping.

Leslie threw her arms in the air. "I can't believe this!"

Tori stared at her blankly before bursting into laughter. "I adore you, but I just chased a thief named after a fictional character through the streets of Manhattan. Every time I've seen you recently, all hell has broken loose. I need a break."

Chapter 20

Buns of Steel

And she meant it. Over the next few weeks, Tori threw herself so deeply into work that she barely spoke with anyone.

That wasn't entirely true. She did make time to pass on her apologies to Derek. They met for drinks, but both quickly realized that outside of some sexual chemistry, they had nothing in common.

Since sex was no longer on the menu, *AGAIN,* Tori looked for a new outlet. Luckily, one of the perks of working at Walker was a free gym membership.

Early one Monday morning, Tori was determined to start her day off with exercise before heading into the office.

"If I work out now, I'm done at six, and I can make it there by 9," she told herself.

Happy endorphins and a bright attitude were just what the doctor ordered because the past few weeks with Diane had been hellish. A few purchase proposals had been sent to clients at Diane's insistence, which was a disaster. Diane wanted to ignore all the complaints, figuring she could turn it around before Errol returned.

Tori saw the writing on the wall. Secret meetings were happening in the office, and for the last few weeks, Roger would storm in, kicking everyone out of the conference room to speak with Diane. Their muffled voices had the office buzzing with gossip.

Tori packed her bag and walked out of her apartment, enjoying the rare quiet moment in the neighborhood before dawn. She nodded at the boys throwing stacks of newspaper from the back of a graffiti-laden truck and the group of crackheads stumbling to their den.

Tori turned the corner, startling an exhausted streetwalker, and smiled as she passed. The woman returned it, sweetness showing behind weary eyes and broken teeth. If not for her God, that could've been her. "I bet my guardian angels are sick of me."

The gym was empty when she walked onto the floor. Tori had picked the perfect time to go. Not a creep in sight. More than once, she complained to security. Their attempts to stop gawkers were feeble at best. One particularly bold guard had asked for her number and gave her an attitude when she said no. *What was the use of going to a gym where even the security guards were hostile?*

After stretching, Tori switched to her workout playlist, a mix of wrestling theme songs, 80s rock, and 90s rap. She hopped on the treadmill at a low 3.2 mph, giving her body time to warm up. Tori zoned out, running until her thighs felt like they were on fire while music blasted against her eardrums at an unsafe level. She had a love-hate relationship with running. Was there a secret link between sadism and exercise? It could be painful, but the endorphins afterward were magical, borderline orgasmic.

The harsh trill of Tori's ringtone interrupted her thoughts, "Who in the hell's calling this early?"

"Darling, are you awake?" a sultry voice asked.

Tori muffled her groan and answered brightly, "Hello, Mother. What are you doing up so early?"

"I figured I would call you. You've been so busy that you haven't seen or spoken to your mother in ages." The woman was an expert at the guilt trip.

Tori calculated how much time had passed since their last conversation, "We spoke three days ago. That hardly counts as an age."

"You're being obtuse," her mother answered, going into a long tirade about Tori's inability to fulfill her filial duties.

It's too early for this! Tori thought, biting her tongue. "OK! You're right, Mother. So has something happened? What do you have going on?"

Tori's mother paused. "Oh, nothing much. I was talking to your Auntie Denise about Tracey's latest accomplishments."

Being an Auntie was a sacred right in Black culture, but as an only child,

Tori's mother's friends became her de-facto Aunts. Auntie Denise was a sweetheart, and her huge family always welcomed them with big arms, but by the time Tori hit her mid-twenties, she put her foot down and refused to claim anyone except for the core group that was a part of raising her. It didn't help that Auntie status could be taken away depending on petty beef. *Yesterday's Auntie might not be today's Auntie, depending on who pissed her mother off.*

"And how are they?" Tori asked dutifully (an unnecessary question, her mother would tell her regardless).

"She's celebrating. Your Aunt is going to be a grandmother for the second time," her mother announced, sighing dramatically.

"Tracey's pregnant? That's fantastic!" Tori was genuinely happy for them. Friends since their first day of middle school, Auntie Denise and her mother reminded Tori of her relationship with Aaliyah.

Behind her father and Tori, Aaliyah was probably her mother's least favorite person in the world. Her mother would be incredibly offended every time Tori made the comparison. Still, Auntie Denise would always roll her eyes and tell another anecdote, happy to finally share the stories that Black mothers promised you could hear when you were "grown." But that same maturity would be held against you when they called you grown for the slightest things but belittled you 'cause they weren't "one of your little friends."

Half the time, the tales were almost identical to Tori's situations with Aaliyah over the years. Her mother's hatred for Aaliyah stemmed from the point that Tori was kicked out of her home. Aaliyah's family took her in despite her mother's protests, an act she had never forgiven.

It wasn't lost on Tori that her mother had taken satisfaction at the thought of her being on the street.

"Yes. Tracey's having her second and is engaged to be married again. It would help if you put yourself out there more," her mother continued. Oh, Fuck! Warmer weather had reawakened her mother's desire for Grandchildren. It was too early for this shit.

"It's too early for this." Tori protested. She knew she shouldn't have answered the phone.

"Victoria, I married at 20 and gave birth to you at 22. You'll be 30 soon; you should be more concerned." Her mother started a familiar argument.

Tori was losing her patience. "I don't know if you remember, but I'm getting divorced. Pretty bad time for a baby."

"Don't be ridiculous, Victoria." Her mother scoffed. "How could I forget? I remember when you called me to tell me you were getting divorced. I thought you were you were pregnant! Another failure."

"Wha--" Tori sputtered. She slowed the treadmill down to give a proper response, but her mother blazed forward.

"I understand if you don't want to get married again, but what about having a baby?"

Jesus! she thought. Tori was in disbelief. What new point of desperation was this?

"You gave me hell for living with Craig before the wedding, and now you want me just to have a kid so you can be a grandma?" she said through gritted teeth. "You know it's not too late for you if you want to have another child." Maybe a sibling would alleviate her mother's disappointment. Tori took an angry gulp of water.

Her words have no power, she reminded herself.

"I still can, you know. If you need a surrogate, I can do it," her mother said.

Tori spit out her water. "Oh, fuck no! Are you kidding?"

"Don't curse at me!" Her mother's shrill tone forced Tori to take out one of her earphones.

"Mother, YOU taught me all these curses." Tori snapped.

"That was different--" her mother started, the familiar excuses at the ready.

Tori cut her off. "You know I should just really focus on my--"

Before she could finish that sentence, she heard a man shout, "Tori!"

"Oh no," she groaned, recognizing Gerard's voice.

He walked over with a smirk on his face. "You haven't answered my calls."

"Honestly, I've been busy, and there's nothing to say." Tori picked up her bottle to walk away.

Gerard grabbed her by the elbow and leaned close, his slight Jamaican accent tickling her ear familiarly. "I can't stop thinking about you."

In her ear, Tori's mother laughed. "Victoria! Who is that?"

Oh shit! She had forgotten her mother was listening.

Tori cleared her throat. "I think we both understand that everything passes its course, but um…" she edged around him. "It was nice running into you!"

"Tori!" he said insistently. "Don't leave like that!"

Gerard leaned his body closer, trailing a finger across her chest. "I get hard if I even think of you."

He looked down, pointing out a very noticeable bulge in the front of his too-tight joggers.

"What the fuck!" she hissed, realizing that the gym was beginning to fill up.

He looked around, noticing an older woman ambling on a machine behind them for the first time.

"Let's go back to my place." He smiled. "We'll have a real workout."

The woman on the treadmill, who'd been eavesdropping the whole time, smirked at them.

"Not a chance," she said firmly, turning away. Tori was hard-pressed to remember why she let herself get involved with him in the first place.

"Don't be like that. We should have dinner and talk it over!" he said, trying to turn on the charm.

She curled her lip in disgust. "I'm not interested. Take care." Tori walked toward the locker room. Her refusal pissed him off, and he followed.

"You say that now, but I know what you like. Do you know what your problem is?" Gerard took her hand. "You're the perfect woman for me...but you're too strong. You'll be alone because you want to be difficult."

Tori felt herself go cold. Craig used to say the same damn thing. It pissed her the fuck off, then. Nothing had changed.

She smiled sweetly. "The fact that you are looking for a weak woman is a sign. I hope you never find one dumb enough to fall for your bullshit."

She pulled her arm out of his grasp and walked away. In her ear, Tori's mother shouted her disapproval, "Was that the man you were seeing? I can't believe he said that to you. And at the gym!"

"You should've seen the bulge. Horny bastard!" Tori laughed, quickly grabbing her bag from the locker and heading to the door. She didn't see him on the way out. *Good Riddance!*

"My God, Victoria," her mother said in shock.

"Exactly. I've got to go." Tori hung up and hurried back home.

Shadow greeted her at the door with a swishing tail and a loud meow. The food bowl was empty.

Feeding the cats, Tori added another note to her to-do list, "Learn to repel assholes immediately."

Chapter 21

The Importance of Being Frank

Tori walked into the office around 8:30, hoping to crack Paris up with a reenactment of Gerard's morning salute at the gym, when Roger stormed out of the conference room.

"Good morning!" Tori said brightly as he passed by her, receiving a grimace in response.

The glass door to the conference room slammed just short of shattering. A clear view of Diane hastily wiping tears from her face in the room that he had exited warned Tori that a storm was brewing.

The last person that said they saw Diane cry was fired for no reason days later, and today, Tori didn't want her good mood ruined by misplaced aggression. She tried to change directions, but Diane noticed her before she could turn away. "Why are you late?" she demanded.

Tori didn't bother looking at the clock. "I'm early…" she answered, "…it's not nine o'clock yet." Diane saw Tori's narrowed eyes and decided not to push her luck.

It was a good decision. Between Tori's mother's surprise surrogacy offer and Gerard's overblown ego, Tori felt like a ticking time bomb.

Diane huffed. "You love making excuses, don't you? Today's going to be a busy day. Meet with everyone on this list and send out the updated packages. I'm leaving."

With that, Diane dropped a stack of files in Tori's hands and walked out of the door toward where her husband stood, talking heatedly into a cell phone.

What the hell? Tori thought, watching them get on the elevator.

Paris strolled over and pulled the list out of her hands. "Trouble in paradise. Have you looked at this list?"

"Not yet. What was that all about, and why are you here so early?" Tori asked, peaking at the list.

"There are some heavy hitters here," he said with a whistle.

She noticed that he looked flushed, as though he had been running.

"Stop avoiding the question. Are you OK?" Tori asked in concern.

"I'm fine. This morning was busy." He wiped his brow and changed the subject. "You and I both know that half of the stuff she wants is already done. You want to sneak out for an early lunch?"

"I would, but...." Tori lowered her voice

"You have to call the lawyer." Paris finished her sentence in exasperation.

"Craig got our dates postponed in court again. He keeps telling the judge that he's away doing volunteer work. My lawyer said it's a bleeding-heart stalling tactic. When I found out, I had Leslie pretend to be a potential client to see if she could get a meeting, and they said he was free that day," Tori said bitterly.

"Sneaky motherfucker. I'm sorry, but this should cheer you up." He pulled her into the conference room. "Take a look!"

Paris opened his phone, sifting through pictures of engagement rings.

"These are gorgeous! This one!" Tori squealed excitedly, pointing to a platinum band with two small channel-set diamonds in the center.

"Ugh! I know you were going to like that. You always pick the plain one." Paris's expression betrayed him. He knew the ring was perfect.

"It's not plain! I don't think your fiancé will want a butterfly-shaped diamond." Tori laughed, looking at a particularly ostentatious ring Paris had put in the pile.

"Yes, the ruggedly handsome boring love of my life." Paris sighed dramatically while Tori rolled her eyes.

"You're so full of shit." Tori was not falling for it today. For all his complaining, Paris and Marco had a special connection.

"I know." Suddenly serious, Paris's eyes glittered. "I lucked out. I'm doing everything that I can to keep him."

Tori raised an eyebrow. "What are you talking about? He adores you."

"Of all people, you know how hard it is to try again after you've been burned. We made the same mistakes. I married the first asshole who told me they loved me after I came out, and he was cut from the same cloth as your ex. I want to get it right this time." Paris shook his head.

"What do you always tell me?" Tori asked with a smile.

"If you cradle the ball--" Paris started with a mischievous grin.

"Not that, asshole," Tori interrupted, laughing. "Marco's not your ex. We can't walk around shut down because of the past."

"I'm glad you said that. I've got a surprise for you." He grinned mischievously. "Ah! Before you give me that face, it's not like when you were out playing Black Doug with Leslie and Hulk."

"Her name is Renee, and technically, I was the ho. Right?" Tori pretended to be ashamed.

"You barely dipped a toe in the ho pool, but my little girl is growing up and hooking up with dangerous men in fancy hotels. You remind me of a slightly younger me. I'm so proud." Paris dabbed a fake tear as Tori hit his arm playfully.

Beaming like he'd come up with a brilliant idea, Paris announced, "I've decided that you're going to keep the momentum going. I made you a dating profile."

"You did what?!" Tori screeched.

"Yep, and you're very popular. You have a date Saturday night. This one isn't from the app, though. I met him at one of those dinners Marco drags me to." Paris took her phone and quickly set a calendar invite with the location.

"No," Tori said. She still hadn't recovered from the last date.

"I'm not taking no for an answer. Either you go, or I'm gonna figure out ways to invite men to every event you attend," he threatened.

Tori raised an eyebrow. "Don't you already do that?"

"Yeah, but from now on, it will be like the dating game in my living room." Paris folded his arms in a challenge.

She shook her head. "Not a chance. I had a bad experience with that in high school with Aaliyah."

"At some point, we'll have to talk more about these weird little side missions you've had your whole life." Paris shook his head. "This one's cute…."

"Great. If I have to sit through another conversation about cryptocurrency…."

"That wasn't even a date. He happened to sit next to you at dinner." Paris huffed.

"Don't give me that." She quipped. "You had already shown the man my picture and told him I was divorced!"

Paris opened the conference door. "I'm not trying to get you re-married, just laid...." He held up his hand before she could protest, "...regularly. You need entertainment, Tori! You can't sit in the house with a dusty pussy because of one bad night."

"Dusty pus–! Imma find some friends who respect me, damn it!" Tori shook her head. "Let's get this shit over with."

Most of their coworkers had arrived when they left the conference room. Paris winked and sauntered away, leaving Tori to tend to the list. She had completed most of this already, so it should be an easy day.

Tori turned the corner, running into Alan, one of Diane's main sycophants. Most of the office was full of decent people, but a small subset was devoted to Diane, playing spy when she wasn't around.

The Rat Pack, as Tori called them, were four bleached blondes with an affinity for dressing like Effie from the Hunger Games. Alan, the only male devotee of the group, nodded in Tori's direction. Clothes aside, he wasn't bad when Diane wasn't around.

"Did she leave?" he asked.

"Mhmm. She mentioned an offsite meeting and gave me a list," Tori answered. It dawned on her that he might know more about the sale. Taking a chance, she adopted a casual tone, asking, "Do you know what the meetings are for?"

"Errol's got her doing something with the investors. She argued with one the other day." He stopped talking, noticing someone over Tori's shoulder. Judy, another of Diane's cronies, joined them with a wicked smile.

"What are you talking about?" she asked, looking at the two like they were conspirators. Judy stepped in between them, deliberately crowding Tori's space.

"Just looking for Diane." Alan stammered. He looked like he wanted the floor to swallow him. *Why was he so on edge?*

Judy pursed her lips. "Yeah, I saw she left in a hurry." She turned a calculating eye toward Tori. "Do you know anything?"

"Nope." Tori chose that moment to make her exit. Whatever drama those two were about to start was not worth it.

She looked at the list again. The only thing she needed to do was call a courier for the sensitive ones. Easy Money.

Her phone dinged with Paris's message: "Here's his number. Be nice." She rolled her eyes and ignored the message. Blind dates were always a bad idea.

Her phone beeped again, a message from the lawyer saying to call immediately. She dialed the number.

"Frank, I got your message. Is it over yet?" she asked hopefully.

"We're going to sit down with him for arbitration soon…" he paused, "…and we may need to do a financial audit."

She sighed. "At this point, I would pay for this to be over with…."

He laughed. "It's not going to come to that, but I'm gonna need more money if arbitration doesn't pan out."

"More money that I don't have…" she started to protest, but Frank cut her off.

"Hey, don't get an attitude with me. You're free to find someone else to take on your ex. I don't need extra headaches from a client." He huffed.

Tori heard the threat in his voice. Frank knew how hard it was for her to find someone decent in the first place.

"There are plenty of ways a girl like you can make some money under the table," he said.

Tori shuddered. "What's that supposed to mean?" she snapped.

"Hey, I'm just being Frank with you." He guffawed at his joke. "You can keep doing the legwork yourself, but if you can swing it, I can have my team on it. You used to have a house, right? Think of it as earnest money."

She groaned. "Frank, you know how much I make. I'm barely

scratching out a living now."

"Divorce is expensive. You're pretty and resourceful. Get a loan." He hung up abruptly.

Great. Another shakedown.

A text popped up from Paris, "Wear something tight tomorrow."

Tori didn't have time for this, but Paris would not take no for an answer. "I'm not expected to bring him to your party, right?" she called him, plotting ways she could wiggle her way out of it.

"No. That was my excuse to make sure you didn't make any other plans. There is a party, but it will be Marco's sexually repressed family. Every time his mother sees me, I swear she gets into a seizure," Paris said sarcastically.

"I thought they were supportive?" From what Tori knew, Marco was really close to his mom.

"Oh, she's not upset that he's gay." He sighed dramatically. "She hates me. She's so conservative that she stood before my artwork and started praying."

"Let me guess...." Tori did a facepalm, "...the full frontal nude in your living room."

"After all those years living in Italy, she should be more cultured. It's art," he said with a huff.

Tori laughed. "I'm not sure a picture of your dick counts as art. Maybe you should cover it with fig leaves à la David."

"They'd be down to my knees." He quipped. "At least she knows how I got him."

"You're incorrigible. Let me work in peace, please." Tori laughed, putting away the phone.

OK, time to make this day fly by. She sent for the courier and started working.

A few hours later, she got a message from her mother inviting her to dinner. Still smarting from their call earlier, Tori almost said no, but thought better of it. Might as well get it over with.

She grabbed her coat to leave but noticed one of the packages was still there. "Why wasn't this sent earlier?" Tori asked.

Poor Lana was frantic. "I've been trying to get a hold of the courier, but no one showed up. I would take it over myself, but I need to pick up my daughter from daycare. I'm already running late."

"Don't worry about it. I'll drop it off." Tori offered.

"Really? That would save my ass." She hesitated. "Are you sure? I don't want to cause any trouble with Diane."

"I've got this." Tori took the box out of her hands. "That reminds me, I have some coloring books for Megan. I'll bring them next week."

"Thank you!" Lana said, rushing out of the door. "I owe you one."

Lana had it rough. Diane had threatened to fire Lana more than once for leaving early, but it couldn't be helped. Her daughter Megan, an adorable gap-toothed toddler, went to daycare that closed by 6. If Lana didn't get there on time, she risked paying fines to the school. Tori tried to cover for her whenever she could after Lana confided that her salary was barely enough to cover their rent. When Lana asked Diane for a raise, she was laughed out of the room.

Ordering an Uber, Tori texted her mother that she would be late.

Twenty minutes later, she arrived on the Upper Eastside. Ringing the doorbell, Tori was buzzed into a gorgeous black marble lobby with dark wood accent furniture. A young woman walked out and greeted her, "How can I help you?"

"I'm just here to drop this off. It's from Walker Art House."

"What's your name?" the woman asked.

"Tori. I work with Diane."

"Hold on one moment." She typed out a message and received a fast reply. "You can go back." Pressing a button under the desk, the double doors behind her opened.

In front of a waterfall wall stood Jonathan, the guy Paris introduced her to at Leslie's party.

"I heard it was you. I wanted to come and see you myself."

Surprised, Tori shook his hand. "Oh, that's very kind of you. I hope you've been well."

"So formal." He noted. "You didn't call."

"You're right." Tori apologized sheepishly. "I've been busy recently."

"No matter. You're here now." He pushed a panel on the wall that she hadn't realized was a door. "Step into my office. I want to talk to you about your future with my company."

"Excuse me?" she raised an eyebrow.

Jonathan nodded curtly. "Might as well take advantage of the time you're here."

Tori followed him into a well-decorated office. "Is this an interview?"

He quirked his lips in a smile. "Everything's an interview. Have a seat."

Chapter 22

Timeo Danaos et Dona Ferentes

Thirty minutes later, Tori sat in the back of an Uber, racing towards the address her mother had sent. Harry's was an upscale lounge in Harlem that Tori had wanted to check out for a while. It was still a little early, but the place had a line wrapped around the corner.

She checked her mother's message. "I'm inside; give them my name." Tori hesitated, looking at the waiting crowd before approaching an official-looking young woman checking a guest list. "Hi, I––"

The hostess took one look at her. "You must be Vivian's daughter."

Tori smiled. "Uh, yeah."

"She's waiting for you on the patio. Maurice, can you take her to the back." The woman unhooked the rope, letting Tori pass through.

"Sure." Maurice smiled. He led her through the room, expertly avoiding being jostled by the crowd. "Nikki said you're Vivian's daughter. I LOOOVE her. I wish she were my mom. You're so lucky."

He opened the door to the patio, and loud music saved her from answering.

As they approached the table, Tori saw a group of men seated around her mother, hanging on her every word with rapt attention. Like a queen addressing her court, Vivian smiled indulgently while they laughed at some joke she made.

"Ms. Vivian! She's here." Maurice beamed.

Vivian, Tori's mother, was a stunning woman with upturned eyes, lashes so long that one could be forgiven for thinking they weren't natural, and flawless mahogany skin that hid her age. Sometimes she looked more like an older sister than her mother.

"And this is my daughter, Victoria," she announced, sliding out of the booth.

She squeezed her arms around her daughter. "My baby," she exclaimed before stepping back with an appraising look.

"Have a seat," Vivian ordered Tori before turning to her admirers. "It was lovely speaking with you, but I MUST catch up with my daughter." A smooth dismissal.

"Maurice, darling. Thank you. Can you bring us a menu and another refill for my glass?" She winked.

Maurice nodded. "Anything for you," he said before hurrying back inside.

"You look disheveled," Vivian asked, reaching a hand out to fix Tori's hair.

Tori tried not to flinch at her touch. "It's been an odd day."

"Mmm." Vivian pursed her lips in disapproval. "So I've heard."

Maurice returned with a bottle of prosecco, "Compliments of the gentleman over there."

Over his shoulder, the group from earlier raised a glass to them.

Vivian smiled. "Please exchange this for a bottle of Cliquot, Brut, not Demi. Thank you."

Tori hid her amusement behind a glass of water on the table.

Tori broke the silence between them. "This place is nice. I haven't been here before." The backyard patio was large, with high cocktail tables and lounge chairs. A DJ booth with an unattended bar was in the corner, and there was a small raised stage with a dance floor in the center. "This would be great to rent for a party," she observed.

"Yes. The governor just hosted an event here." Vivian pursed her lips. "If you'd been on time, you would have met the owner."

Tori heard the rebuke in her voice. "I apologize. It was unexpected." She looked around the room, avoiding her mother's glare.

"Victoria, are you going to tell me why you were late?" her mother's tone told her there better be a good excuse.

She sighed. "I had an interview. "

"With whom?" Vivian asked; her nonchalant tone didn't match the calculating gleam in her eyes.

Tori hesitated. *Should I tell her?* It was probably safer not to, but she didn't want to lie. "It's a friend of Paris. He's looking for someone to work with his collection."

"I don't understand. Why would he want you?" her mother asked incredulously.

Always the tone of disbelief. Tori tried to keep the annoyance out of her voice, "Why? I'm very good at what I do. He saw some of my work, and Paris introduced us a few weeks ago."

Her mother curled her lip. "That abomination. You spend too much time around his kind." Her eyes narrowed. "Is there something you haven't told me?"

Tori looked at her quizzically. "His kind? If you wanted me to hate gay people, you shouldn't have sent me to an all-girl school."

She grabbed Tori's wrist, gripping it tightly. "Don't play with me."

"Jesus!" Tori winced and pulled her arm away, resisting the urge to rub the bruise.

184

"Don't take the Lord's name in vain." Vivian hissed. "I didn't raise you to be an embarrassment––"

Tori cut her off. "Jesus loves everyone." Her mother started her familiar anti-gay tirade, but Tori stopped her. "Don't worry, Mother. I haven't forgotten your rules."

Don't be a stripper, Don't embarrass me. Don't be a dyke. Vivian used to scream at Tori in between beatings.

Vivian didn't hate gay men. She spent years working with them. Some she even mentored, only calling them names and sneering behind their backs. It was fear of lesbians that made Vivian lose sleep at night. She watched Tori's female friendships closely, afraid that some exposure had planted a seed in her. "I'll do you like Marvin Gaye's father," her mother would threaten.

Maurice came back with the right bottle. "I love how you did that, Ms. Vivian."

"Knowing your worth is everything, darling," she winked. "Victoria, Maurice just graduated with honors from NYU."

Tori smiled. "Congratulations, that's wonderful. What was your major?"

"Poli-sci," he said proudly. "Your mom said she can introduce me to a few people in the Mayor's office."

"Yes." Vivian nodded sagely. "Maurice has a bright future. Make sure you give me your number before we leave."

Adoration for Vivian shone out of his eyes as he blushed prettily. Her mother had an incredible ability to draw people out of their shells. When Vivian turned on the full radiance of her smile, you felt like you were the luckiest person in the world to receive her attention. Tori hadn't seen one pointed her way for quite a while.

"Maurice!!!" someone called out.

"Oops, I've got to see the other tables, but I'll be back. Thank you so much, Ms. Vivian!" Maurice hurried away.

"He seems nice," Tori noted as she sipped from her glass.

Vivian nodded. "He's a brilliant young man. Too bad he's gay."

"What does that have…never mind." Tori dropped the subject. She didn't come here for an argument.

"I've got something for you." Her mother slid a small jewelry box across the table.

Surprised, Tori opened it. Inside was a small pearl pendant necklace. It was beautiful. "Wow. This is lovely. Thanks, Mom."

"My pleasure…" Vivian smiled. "Now you don't have to wear that awful…."

A man interrupted her, "Excuse me, Vivian. Would you like to dance?" He was handsome, with large, fake, impossibly white teeth. The man appeared in his early 50s and was well-dressed in a nice pair of slacks and a blazer.

Tori smiled. "Go ahead, Mom. I'll hold your purse."

He led Vivian to the dance floor, but he was sorely outmatched. The poor man did a stiff two-step while Vivian twirled around him. She was naturally graceful, and her poor partner, no doubt recognizing his comparative inadequacies, was quickly left on the sidelines. A circle formed around Vivian, hyping her up as she spun lithely. She signaled Tori to join her in the crowd. Tori grabbed their purses and met her mother on the dance floor.

"You brought the bags? Wait here." Vivian walked to the DJ booth, greeting him with a kiss. After a quick conversation, she tucked them behind his equipment and danced back to her.

Tori raised an eyebrow in confusion. "An old friend," Vivian yelled in her ear over the music.

The crowd pressed in tighter around them as more people began to dance. The DJ was good. Soon Tori lost herself in the music. She looked at her mother and smiled; Vivian was in her element. This brought back fun childhood memories of dancing together in the house. Tori had been terrible at it for a long time. All Vivian's attempts to teach her ended in bruised toes and peals of laughter. They joked that her rhythm kicked in when her hips developed. Tori would never be a pro, but she could hold her own.

Tori looked at her watch, realizing they had been on the floor for hours. She tapped her mother on the shoulder. "I'm going to sit down for a sec."

"I'll join you!" Vivian smiled apologetically to the guy she was dancing with and followed Tori to the table.

Maurice had placed a reserved sign, keeping the table free for them.

"That was fun. I need a new shirt." Tori pulled her top away from her sweaty body while they poured from the bottle on the table.

"I love a good workout." Vivian dabbed at her skin gently with a napkin.

"Mom, don't look now. The guy from earlier is staring at you." Tori giggled.

Vivian laughed. "Big teeth? He had terrible breath. The only thing he can do for me is buy another bottle."

"Coldblooded." Tori chuckled.

"Victoria, I haven't forgotten about the fool I heard on the phone this morning." Her mother raised an eyebrow.

Tori winced. "Really? I want to pretend that never happened. I can't stop thinking about the interview earlier, but the timing isn't great."

"What about the divorce?" Vivian asked as she inspected her glass.

"We have court next week. Frank said I shouldn't switch jobs until this is over, but he asked for more money," Tori explained. "I told Leslie that I'd pay alimony to be done--"

Vivian interrupted, "Don't be stupid." She shook her head. "I can't believe you let any of this--"

Tori was steaming. "Let what, Mom? Which part? The part where he's trying to bleed me dry or the part where we kept fighting?"

Vivian scoffed. "Had I known what was going on––"

"What would you have done?" Tori demanded. She knew coming here was a bad idea. It was the same argument every time.

Vivian scoffed. "I've never let anyone else get away with putting their hands on you."

She doesn't even see anything wrong with that statement. Tori looked down at the table as she listened to Vivian list all the reasons she had never liked Craig—total bullshit. "My darling future son-in-law," Vivian declared the moment they met. The feeling wasn't exactly mutual on his part.

"Are you paying attention?" Vivian rapped her hand again.

Startled, Tori realized her mother had stopped talking. "I have to go to the ladies' room."

She hurried away from the table and into the restroom.

Tori stared in the mirror. "Dry your eyes and pick your battles." She steeled herself and walked back to the table.

On her approach, she saw "Big Teeth" had returned to the table and was handing her mother a business card. He kissed her hand, winked at Tori, and walked away with a swagger in his step.

"Can't leave you alone for 2 minutes?" she laughed, trying to lift the mood.

"You exaggerate," Vivian answered primly.

"Madame," the waiter interrupted, offering the check to Vivian.

"My daughter is treating me," she announced, sliding the bill across the table to Tori. "I've called the car."

Got me again! Tori paid without protest, noting Vivian's good mood as she slowly reapplied lipstick before leaving the restaurant.

Their goodbyes were a blur as Tori thought about her mother's words in the back of a cab before calling Paris. She filled him in on the meeting with Jonathan and dinner with her mother, leaving out most of Vivian's anti-gay rant.

"Ms. Vivian is one of a kind. Did she leave you with the check again?" Paris joked.

Tori sighed. "Do you really have to ask?"

"It's OK to say no, you know that—right?" he groaned.

Tori sucked her teeth. "Last time I told her no about something, she came to my old job and beat me up."

"Bitch, you're lying!" Paris exclaimed.

"Why do you think I won't tell her where the office is?" Tori looked at the driver, who was pretending not to eavesdrop. "Shit. I'm still not comfortable with her knowing where I live."

He laughed. "She reminds me of one of my gay-hating aunts. Fabulous but vicious at the same time. Too bad for my aunt, though... she doesn't know her husband, and I had a thing before they met."

"Your UNCLE?!"Tori snickered, "I feel like your family inspired Dynasty."

"Amongst other things." Paris sighed. "Boo, you need a reset—new everything. When the divorce is final, go on vacation. Don't tell your mother until you're getting on the plane."

"I'm planning on it," Tori promised.

Chapter 23

It's a Small World

"I t's nice. Lots of trees."

She looked out the window at the quickly darkening sky. That's odd. It wasn't supposed to rain. The forecast had called for a perfectly sunny 85-degree summer day.

"I haven't had a chance to meet everyone yet, but group activities start in an hour...."

The door opened, and laughter rang through the hallway as a girl entered the room.

"Mommy, I've got to go. Yes. I'll call you after."

"No, I'm not rushing you. They're calling us. Yes. Love you too."

Tori hung up with a groan.

"Your parents?" the girl asked with a grin.

Tori nodded. "My mother. She's upset that they wouldn't let parents stay."

The girl laughed. "Mine too. I'm Nikki."

"Tori." She extended a hand but was pulled in for a hug. She's friendly.

"Five minutes!" a voice called on the other side of the door.

"Do you care which bed I take?" Nikki asked, dropping her bags on an empty desk.

Tori looked around at the sparse dorm room; two twin-sized beds sat on either side with a window separating them. The walls, colossal concrete blocks in the shade of eggshell, glistened wetly as though the paint hadn't dried. It looked like a prison cell without decoration, but none of that mattered; they were only there for the weekend. Classes wouldn't start for another month.

"No. Whichever you prefer."

Tori was just excited to be there. College was going to be amazing. She hadn't wanted to apply to this school, but her mother's desire to keep her close to home won out. She got accepted into one of their dual degree programs with a scholarship that covered everything except room and board. That was no biggie; once her mother paid the three grand, she would officially be a college freshman. Tori was lucky, one of her friends from high school was also going, and they had already agreed to be roommates. The next four years were going to be a breeze.

She watched Nikki unpack. "Wow. You brought a lot of stuff for two nights."

"An outfit for every activity. I want them to look forward to seeing me around." Nikki laughed as she sorted through her things.

Tori glanced at the schedule. "Looks like orientation is first."

"Let's skip to the fun parts," Nikki asked, grabbing the list. *"Freshman mixer at dinner. I'm calling first dibs."*

Someone knocked at the door before stepping into the room.

"I'm Tatiana, your group leader. Y'all ready?"

They followed her out of the room, rejoining the rest of the group.

Tatiana introduced everyone, promising to show them the who's who on campus. When they reached the auditorium, Tatiana had put everyone at ease.

The day was full of team building with previews of classes and activities they could take to entertain them before dinner. Tori didn't care. She was almost in college—no more being under her mother's roof and one step closer to living the dream. Tori half-listened as they droned on and on about the coursework. She wasn't worried; school was easy. Tori had been an honor student her whole life.

"See anyone you like yet?" Nikki asked, watching a group of boys sitting across from them.

"I didn't look. I have a boyfriend," Tori answered.

"More for me." Nikki winked.

Tatiana laughed. "Girl, we've got some fine ass men on campus, but I don't know...some of them are a trip. You might wanna wait."

"Mhmm," Tori agreed. She wondered what Trey, her boyfriend, was doing now. Knowing him, Trey was probably knee-deep in weird video games with his Xbox friends. His mother swore he barely left the house unless he was with her.

Nikki jostled her elbow, alerting her to a few smiles thrown their way by a group of boys in the audience while the Dean of Students announced that the show was about to start. "We've got something really exciting for you today. Please give a round of applause for our Student Union as they present "Staying Safe," a cautionary guide for incoming first-year students."

"Ooo, who's that?" Nikki asked.

"Stay away from that one," Tatiana whispered.

On stage, a boy pretended to be a jock at a party, spiking his date's drink before leading her to his room with loud hooting from the other actors.

What kind of school is this? Tori wondered.

She looked around at the bored faces of her soon-to-be classmates, but no one else seemed alarmed. Maybe it's just me.

Tatiana walked them back to the room when it was over, saying, "The upper-level students are throwing a party in an hour. Y'all should come."

"We'll be there!" Nikki volunteered as they waved goodbye. She chattered away excitedly as she looked through Tori's bag. The girl had no sense of

personal space.

"*Do you have a roommate planned already?*" *Nikki asked, holding Tori's clothes against her in the mirror.*

"*Yeah. One of my friends is also coming to the school, but she had to go away for a family trip this weekend,*" *Tori said as she put away the stuff Nikki had thrown haphazardly across the bed.*

Nikki looked disappointed. "*Oh, OK. Maybe we could be roommates if that doesn't work out?*"

"*If anything changes, I'll let you know,*" *she said aloud.*

HELL NO! Tori thought.

Nikki would probably drive her up the wall if today were anything to go by.

Nikki started picking out her outfit, leaving Tori alone. If Tasha came to the school, it wouldn't be necessary. It was partially her fault that Tori was there. If it were up to her, she would be so far away no one from home would ever find her. Egypt was her first choice until Tasha mentioned the school in front of Tori's mother.

"*I don't want to stay in Jersey. If you would look at the brochure....*" *Tori never got to finish the sentence.*

Vivian ripped up the application and backhanded her across the mouth. "*You're not fucking going over there. You're too stupid. You'll be lucky if I let you go anywhere.*"

"But I can..." she started before Vivian grabbed her by the throat, smacking Tori's face into the dining room table. "Yes, Mommy," she whimpered.

"Hellllooooo! Earth to Tori...you spaced out like Raven," Nikki laughed. "You seeing the future?"

More like the past, she thought.

Tori lied. "Sorry, I was deciding what to wear."

"Mhmm...I'm gonna hop in the shower. I'll be ready in a few." Nikki grabbed her things and walked out, leaving Tori alone with her thoughts.

She started to call her mother back but thought better of it. "I can just tell her they kept us busy."

Lightning illuminated the sky outside as Tori stared out of the window again. This place was the perfect setting for a slasher movie. A sense of foreboding came over her.

What is wrong with me tonight? She wondered, dismissing it as nerves. She looked at her bag and decided against changing just as Nikki returned. *Might as well get this over with.*

"You're going in that?" Nikki asked with a grimace as she put on her shoes.

"Yeah." Tori looked down at her outfit. "I don't want to stay for long."

"Fine." Nikki rolled her eyes. "Let's go."

The party was packed by the time they arrived. Teenagers ran through the *hallway, laughing and chasing each other while music bumped inside the room. The upperclassmen dorms were way nicer than the cell they were staying in. A makeshift bar was set up in one corner, with a long line taking turns pouring drinks from the punch bowl.*

"Y'all made it!" *Tatiana ran over, giving them each a hug.*

"Yo, T! Who are these lovely ladies?" *A boy walked over, throwing an arm around Tatiana.*

"I'm Nikki." *She stepped forward with a grin.*

"Girl, you look like an angel." *The boy smiled, kissing her hand.*

"You got a name?" *Nikki asked, smiling coyly.*

"Donovan, leave my girls alone and go bother someone else." *Tatiana swatted him playfully.*

"Damn, girl. You ain't gotta blow up my spot like that." *Donovan winked and walked away.* "Don't forget me, Nikki. I'll see you later."

"I won't!" *she called after him.*

Tatiana laughed. "Don't pay him any mind. He has a girl. Y'all walk around and say hi. I'll catch up with you in a sec." *She walked away, greeting other newcomers to the party.*

Nikki nudged her. "There he is."

"Who?" *Tori asked.*

Nikki pointed to the left. "The guy from earlier. From the play."

It took a second for Tori to remember what she was talking about.

"Mr. Date Rape?" she asked but didn't get an answer. When she turned, Nikki smiled at a different boy standing near the punch bowl. He waved her over.

"I'll be back," Nikki said, walking toward him.

Great. Definitely never going to be roommates with her. Tori sighed. I'll walk around for 10 minutes, then leave.

She slowly made her way around the room. A shelf of video games in the corner and a few textbooks on the desk gave no real clues about the owner. She looked down at her watch, "five minutes to go."

At that moment, a guy appeared in front of her. "You in a rush?"

Tori looked up; Oh shit! It's Mr. Date Rape. She laughed nervously. "Kinda."

"Too bad. Welcome to my room. I'm Craig." He reached out a hand.

She shook it reluctantly, feeling like she'd been caught. "Tori."

He was taller than her, heavy set with hazel eyes, faint pockmark scars, and a cocky grin. "You coming here in September?" He leaned in close, clouding her senses with the smell of cheap body spray.

"Yep." She looked around him toward the door.

"Only one-word answers?" He narrowed his eyes and thrust a cup into her hand. "Here, have this."

Tori looked down at the cup and was immediately filled with dread. "Uh, thanks, but I've got to go."

She turned and hurried to Nikki. "Hey, I need to go back to the room. Are you ready?

"Now? We just got here! I'm gonna stick around." Nikki poured another cup.

"Are you sure? I don't want to leave you with––" Tori glanced over her shoulder toward Craig, but he was nowhere to be found.

"Yeah. I'm good." Nikki cut her off impatiently, signaling toward the boy from the punch bowl.

Tori caught the hint. She nodded and walked away, only stopping to say goodbye to Tatiana and ask her to keep an eye on Nikki.

The rain had stopped by the time she got back to the room. Tori looked at the cup she had carried from Craig's room without drinking and walked to the bathroom to pour it out. She watched the liquid swirl down the drain, feeling like she'd just dodged a bullet when her ringtone pulled her out of her sleep.

Tori woke up in bed and answered the phone groggily, "Morning, Daddy."

"Morning? It's afternoon, kiddo. You were asleep?" her father laughed.

She looked at the clock; 12:30 *already?*

"Yeah, I was out with Mom last night and didn't get in until late." Tori sat up, shaking the dream off.

"I'm sure that's a story." He laughed. "Just wanted to make sure we're still on for dinner tomorrow."

"Of course! I'll cook." Tori and her father had a standing dinner date every month. "Bring your poker chips."

Her father groaned. "Oh, no. You're not kicking my ass this time, kid. I have to go, but I'll be there early tomorrow. Love you!"

"Love you too, Daddy!" she answered before he hung up.

She sat back in bed, staring at the ceiling before calling Aaliyah on FaceTime.

"G'Day, Mate!" said Aaliyah when she picked up.

Tori chuckled. "You been watching Crocodile Dundee again?"

"You know me so well. What's up? How was dinner with Ms. Vivian? Did you tell her I said hi?" Aaliyah laughed, dropping the accent.

"If I told her that, she'd rip my head off." Tori laughed. "Dad just woke me up from a nightmare."

Aaliyah guessed. "The one with the trees that turned into vibrators?"

"Nope. First-year orientation," Tori said somberly.

"Ahh…" Aaliyah nodded sagely. "He who shall not be named."

Tori grunted. "That's the one."

"Isn't today…" Aaliyah stopped, unwilling to finish her sentence.

Tori looked at the calendar. "Well, that explains a lot. Happy Anniversary to me."

"I'm sorry, Mama." Aaliyah's sad expression touched her.

"No need," Tori answered. "Paris badgered me into a blind date tonight."

Aaliyah snickered. "Hopefully, it's better than the last one."

"You mean the time you tricked me into a double date with the stinky motherfucker 'cause your mom wouldn't let you go solo?" Tori grimaced at the memory. The boy smelled awful and wouldn't stop trying to feel her up in the back seat. She had cursed Aaliyah out so severely that Aaliyah ended the date early.

"Thanks for taking one for the team." Aaliyah laughed.

Tori rolled her eyes. "Mhmm…you STILL owe me for that."

"Put it on my tab. Shit, one of my patients is buzzing me." Aaliyah looked over her shoulder. "Call me after your date?"

"Might need you to get me out of it," Tori answered, only half-kidding.

"Gotcha. Wait! Mr. Walker! WHERE ARE YOUR PANTS!?" Aaliyah shouted as she ended the call.

She thought about the dream again. Craig had sworn he didn't remember speaking to her at the party. Another lie. Two of his friends confessed a few years later that he had explicitly told Tatiana to invite her and Nikki to the room.

Tori looked at the calendar again and sighed; ten years since they first met. Maybe she was turning over a new leaf. Tori had genuinely forgotten their anniversary was this weekend, or she would never have agreed to go out with Paris's mystery guy.

"Can't use that as an excuse, though; it's all about moving on," she said as she searched her closet.

A few hours later, Tori walked into the restaurant.

Great, I'm here first. Maybe he won't show, she thought.

"Victoria?" by the bar, a male voice called her name. She stood near the entrance, frozen in shock, as he hopped down and walked over. "Wow! You're tall!" He looked up at her and grinned.

Tori almost ran out of the restaurant. The man looked exactly like Craig, except she towered over him by 6 inches.

"You're Marcus?!" she asked before recovering, "Um, that's the first time I've been called tall."

"You can call me Big. Come sit." He grinned and walked back over to the bar stool.

BIG?! Was that a joke? Bemused, Tori followed him and sat down. *I'm going to kill Paris,* she thought.

He signaled to the bartender and asked for a menu.

"We'll have the chicken and another drink for me," he told the bartender before handing the menu back.

"Wait!" Tori was confused. "I didn't get a chance to order anything."

"No need. I ordered for us. You'll love it," Marcus answered smugly.

This was not going to go well.

He looked her over. "Paris didn't tell me you were like this."

"Excuse me?" she asked.

"You're better looking than I thought you'd be." Marcus bit his lip and winked.

She suppressed a grimace. "I see. He didn't tell me anything about you, Marcus."

"It's Big, and if you play your cards right, I might let you find out why they call me that." He winked again, to Tori's horror.

The bartender walked over and set a drink down in front of Marcus.

"Rum and coke for you, sir, and what can I get you?" he asked, glancing between them.

The hell out of here, she thought. Tori watched Marcus lick the rim of the glass while staring at her. "Water, please." This was going to be a very short date. No pun intended.

The bartender looked at her sympathetically and walked away.

"So tell me about yourself," Marcus asked.

Tori nodded. "Uh, Paris is a good friend of mine. I recently moved back to the city. I am in the process of getting a divorce."

"Divorced? Why'd you get put back on the shelf?" he asked.

"Excuse me?" Tori's hand gripped the bar to stop herself from slapping him.

"Oh, it's just, you know, you're in your 30s. If you're already divorced, something has to be wrong with you." Marcus slurped his drink as the bartender put a plate of chicken before him.

At his words, the bartender froze and looked at her.

Tori was fuming. "That's a wild thing to say to someone you don't know."

"My bad. I recently went through a breakup. I'm not trying to be rude." Marcus didn't look sorry at all.

I can't imagine why, she thought.

"I'm very sorry to hear that," Tori said politely, looking at the clock.

Five minutes and I'm out of here, she assured herself.

"Yeah, actually, today is her birthday," Marcus said before he burst into sloppy tears.

Embarrassed, she sought help, signaling the bartender to bring over some tissue.

What in the fuck was happening? The bartender, who had been eavesdropping, was trying so hard not to laugh that his shoulders shook.

"Ohhh uhh, here. Don't cry." She handed him the tissue and watched him blow his nose like a trumpet.

"I'm sorry. It's just still hard for me. I was in love." He cried louder as people at the bar turned to look at him.

A perfect out, Tori tried for sympathy. "Well, perhaps you should reach out to her. How long were you together?"

"2 months." He wailed, tearing into the chicken in front of him with his fingers.

She looked at him incredulously. It was time to go. "Well, you should contact her and see if the two of you can work it out."

"You know…" Marcus sniffled, "…you're nice and pretty. Maybe you can fix my broken heart."

"Wait, what?" Tori couldn't believe the speed he went from crying to flirting. The bartender came over with her water and stood there openly watching the scene.

Marcus licked his fingers. "Come home with me. I'll eat you like a Thanksgiving plate."

Tori coughed and spat her water across the room. "I've gotta go." She stood and grabbed her purse as Marcus hopped down from the stool.

He launched himself at her for a hug and buried his head in her chest. "If you're not busy later, you can take me up on my offer."

Peeling herself out of his arms, Tori twisted her face into the closest thing to a smile she could manage and hurried out of the door.

Before she could get outside, she heard his voice. "Hey, I'll walk with you."

Fuck! She braced herself as he ran behind her.

Marcus tried to throw an arm over her shoulder but couldn't. "Slow down, girl. I like my women with long legs."

Is this motherfucker serious! Tori thought as she increased her speed, hoping that his little legs wouldn't be able to keep up.

To her dismay, he managed. "What train are you taking?" she asked.

"The B, downtown," Marcus answered, still trying to put an arm around her. "I'm going to listen to a podcast on the way home. There's a good one called Small Brainz that—-"

That was enough for her."Well, I need to take the 2 Uptown. Get home safely!" Tori ran off, zigzagging through the crowd to escape him, and hurried back outside. She ordered an Uber; thankfully, one was a few feet away.

Tori hopped in and called Paris. "I'm gonna strangle you!"

Paris groaned. "It couldn't have been that bad!"

"He looked just like my ex, was shorter than me, and had the nerve to be a jackass." Tori scolded him.

"First, there's nothing wrong with being short, but he was at least 6 feet." He tried to defend himself.

"Ain't no damn way. I wore flats, and he called me tall Paris. TALL!" she screeched.

As she described the date, Paris cackled. "You know what? When we met, he was standing on the stairs, and I had been drinking. Girl, my bad."

"I hate you, Paris." Tori was over it. "Never-a-fucking-gain."

"You love me…" he laughed, "…at least this wasn't your worst anniversary."

She couldn't even disagree with him on that.

Chapter 24

Daddy Lessons

Tori jumped up when the buzzer rang, startling Shadow in the process. The poor cat lived in a constant state of alarm.

"Oops. Sorry!!" Tori apologized as she sprinted to answer the door. "Daddy!"

"Baby Girl!" Tori heard as her father stepped into the apartment. He ducked, narrowly missing hitting his head on the frame. "I come bearing gifts." He put down a large bag of groceries and spun Tori around in a bear hug.

"What's this? I already cooked." Tori peeked in the bag. Yes! He had picked up some of her favorites. Whenever her dad came over, he would bring something to stock up her cabinets. William Rose, a large man who loved cooking, believed an empty cabinet was a sin.

He smiled as he unpacked the bag. "I was in the store and figured you might like these."

Her father handed her a stack of scratch-off lottery tickets from his pocket. "Here's a quarter. I missed you, kiddo."

Tori laughed. "Missed you too. I'm sorry I haven't been around much. I've been keeping to myself recently."

"After an attempted kidnapping, you should probably stay in the house," her father said gravely.

"You've got that right." Tori avoided his eyes as she set the table. "Don't worry; I'm grounding myself."

"Good. You don't need to sign up for round two with an international criminal," he cautioned.

Tori had already told him the whole story. For all they had been through together, there was no one she trusted more. Among his many virtues, her dad always tried to offer a balanced opinion even if he didn't like what she had to say. It was a trait that Tori appreciated, not to say they hadn't had their share of disagreements. No matter how angry they were with each other, there was an unspoken pact between them that they could talk about anything freely.

She leaned over and hugged him. "Thanks, Daddy. Enough about my walk on the wild side; let me tell you how your wife is driving me nuts?" She gave him a sly grin.

He grimaced. "What did she do now?"

Tori filled him in on her mother's most recent antics. "...and she left me with the check...AGAIN."

Her dad shook his head. "That's your fault. I told you next time she tried that mess to tell her to get ready to wash dishes."

Even though it was almost 15 years since her parents split, neither had taken steps to get a legal divorce. There was something to be said about her parents/grandparents' generation; when they said" I Do," they meant that shit. It did not matter if you were drunk, abusive, a cheater, etc., you could leave, but divorce was virtually unheard of.

Tori was the first in her line to go through with it.

Her grandfather on her mother's side had been married three times and never divorced. In a plot twist, she discovered he got around detection by finding three women with the same name in 3 states. Grandpa Victor had been a smooth-talking giant of a man with a mischievous grin, a devout heart, and a wicked temper. Her grandfather and mother had a terrible relationship born of a deep sense of abandonment, but for all his flaws, she missed him. It wasn't lost on Tori that Vivian had chosen to repeat the same cycle with her child. At least Tori had her father for balance.

Her dad was like an oversized teddy bear with a kind smile and personality to match. He didn't raise his voice, didn't smoke, hell, she barely remembered him finishing a beer until she was an adult. Even her friends called him dad, many expressing their desire to include him as an extra grandparent in an emergency. Tori couldn't imagine life without him.

Fear filled her mind at the thought, and she hugged him again.

Concerned, he asked, "What's wrong, kiddo?"

She pulled away. "Nothing."

Tori laughed awkwardly. "Jeez, I can't hug my favorite person?"

"You can get all the hugs you need, but you can't dodge my question. Talk to me." Tori's father sat her down sternly, the food on the table forgotten.

Tori sighed. "I'm tired of complaining."

He rolled his eyes. "Tori, you're not complaining. I asked. If you don't talk, I can't help."

"This isn't something you can help with, Dad. Every time I try to wiggle my way out of a bad situation, something worse is after it. I can't feel like a passenger in my own life. This divorce is exhausting; my boss has been treating me like shit; I can't sleep, and every time I try to date, it ends in disaster, and Mom is…being Mom. This week, I got some good news, but it doesn't feel real. I don't want to fuck up my life any more than it already is." she vented.

Her father was confused. "Where did you get that from?"

Tori shook her head. "Dad, nothing in my life is going well. According to Frank, taking this new job might be a mistake 'cause Craig will flip if he finds out."

"Kiddo, you're talking in circles. What new job?" he asked.

Realizing she hadn't mentioned it to him, Tori filled her father in, "I had a surprise interview and got an offer on Friday, and I can't stop thinking about it."

"That's great news," he beamed. "Is it a step up?"

"I'd go from a Manager to a Director. I can't even believe they're considering me for this. You normally need a degree." Tori got up, pacing the room anxiously.

"They must know talent when they see it. Stop worrying about the piece of paper. The job is a no-brainer. Why are you so upset?" her father asked.

" I don't know if any decisions I've made are right. Everything is hanging on by such a thin thread now that I'm scared to make another mistake." Tori's voice broke as she held back tears.

He stopped and held her hand. "Didn't I tell you everything will work out? You've got to have a little faith in yourself."

She wiped her eyes. "I know, but--"

Her father interrupted. "Tori, we never talked about what came up in court." He hesitated. "Why didn't you come to me when he put his hands on you?"

Tori sighed. "I got myself into that situation. Having anyone else involved would've made things worse. There was nothing you could have done that he and I hadn't already done to each other."

"You're my daughter." He shook his head. "I'd have broken every bone in his body if I knew."

"Hence my choice. You taught me how to figure things out on my own. I'm not proud of it, but Craig found out the hard way that you taught me a mean right hook." Eager to change the subject, she grabbed the remote. "Want to watch A Patch of Blue or Viva Las Vegas?

"Hey," he stopped her. "Don't shut down on me. You can't keep everything bottled up. It's not healthy."

She blinked at him."Pot meet kettle. You do the same thing, and I didn't invite you over for a cryfest." She scrolled through movie titles, avoiding his eyes.

He nudged her. "Maybe that's what you need."

She grunted, unwilling to answer, "Dad, can I ask you a question?"

"Always." He smiled.

Tori hesitated. "How did you move on after Mom left?"

He sat back and studied her for a moment. "We've never talked about this."

She felt terrible. "I'm sorry. I shouldn't have--"

"No. It's fine." Tori's father chose his words carefully. "It wasn't easy.

When your mother decided to move out, she sent you down south for the summer. We put you on the plane, and she left me as soon as you were in the air. By the time I realized neither of you were coming back, I was in a dark place."

She wiped her eyes. "I remember. First, Grandma died, and then y'all put me on a plane two days later. I never got to say goodbye to her...or you."

He focused on the ground avoiding her eyes. "Your mother thought it was for the best."

"Of course she did," Tori said bitterly. "Best to keep me from the funeral, or best for her to show up two weeks later and tell me I was never coming home?"

He sighed. "It broke my heart, but I thought fighting things would make it worse."

She glared at him. "For a long time, I resented you. I never understood why you didn't want me."

Her father was shocked. "Tori! That was never the case. Our neighborhood was getting worse. I got mugged at gunpoint outside our door a few weeks after you were gone. Besides, your mother--"

"My mother..." she interrupted bitterly, "Spare me. Even if I wanted to lay this all at her feet, I can't. YOU were an adult. There was not one point where you tried to get custody, even when she kicked me out. Do you remember what you said when I begged you to come to see me?"

"Tori, I––" he tried to interject, but she was on a roll.

"You told me to make an appointment. An appointment! I wasn't a client. I was your 15-year-old, and you let me stay with the woman who pulled a gun on you and beat me every other day, or did you block that out?!" Tori knew she was yelling, which wouldn't solve anything.

He looked at her patiently, waiting for her to get these feelings off her chest.

She took a deep breath. "Dad, I-I'm sorry for yelling. I'm not angry with you. I just don't understand. Was it that easy to walk away?"

"You have a right to be angry, and I'm sorry I ever said that." He shook his head. "Do you remember when your mother called the police on me?"

Tori remembered watching her father being led out of the house by police officers after he intervened while Vivian choked her. Her 8-year-old mind couldn't grasp why they were taking him away when her mother had done something bad again. Afraid to speak up, she grabbed Scooby, her favorite bear. She ran to him just as he walked out of the door, pressing the bear into his arms, "So you won't be alone," she whispered, knowing her mother was standing behind her.

"I remember. It's wrong, but I can't imagine how hard it was not to lose your temper." She confessed. "She broke almost every dish we had on your head."

"There were moments where it was hard not to. I'd come home and see you with welts on your legs. I couldn't understand why." He looked at her with tears. "You were so small, and she had so much anger in her. I would pull her off you, and she'd call the cops and make me leave. The only thing that stopped them from arresting me was that she would admit I never put my hands on her. I had a choice, protect you as best as possible or risk going to jail. Then you wouldn't have a father at all."

Tori was ashamed of her outburst. "I'm sorry. I never thought of it like that. Your hands were kinda tied, huh."

"Your mother..." he hesitated, "...she went through a lot before we met, and that doesn't excuse any of it. I know it's hard to believe this, but she loves you."

"Not in a way that's healthy." She shook her head. "I can't remember a week going by without her beating me or telling me I was stupid, ugly, or worthless until she kicked me out of the house in the rain and told me never to come back. I was 17. Don't tell me that's love."

He sighed. "Tori, I know it wasn't fair, but we want the best for you. When your mother and I were kids, everyone got—"

"No. You think I don't know what she went through? I've been forgiving her my whole life because I couldn't imagine how hard she had it." Tori shook her head angrily. "But Mom had a choice just like I did. I'm not y'all. I can't force myself to stay miserable trying to fit into who she wants me to be. And please don't preach to me about forgiving her. It would be easier if I hated her, and she knows that. She takes advantage of me every time I let her back in. She's nice at first, but it never lasts. I'm back to being a "worthless piece of shit" when Mom doesn't get what she wants." She wiped tears away from her eyes.

"Dad, there were moments when I was with Craig," she whispered, remembering her shame, "We would fight, and I'd catch myself throwing something. Chip off the old block, huh."

He groaned. "You can't beat yourself up for defending--"

She shook her head. "I fed into it. We've both physically damaged each other, but it seemed so normal. Even now, I feel like I failed a little by being unable to tough it out. Whenever Craig hurt me, I tried harder to prove I could take it. That I wouldn't give up on him. It was like--"

"The pain brought you closer?" He shook his head. " I felt the same way with your mother, and I wasn't perfect. I thought our problem was money, so I gambled, hoping everything would be fixed if I had enough. It just drove the wedge further between us. I didn't understand what postpartum depression was. I tried to support her dreams, but I didn't know how to communicate, and she didn't know how to listen. I look at you sometimes and see that same chip on your shoulder that she has. I know where it comes from. Even when you were little, you had to tiptoe around our bullshit. You had to act like an adult when there was no safe space, and that's my failure as your father."

"There goes that word again." Tori's voice wavered. "Failure seems like the only thing I'm good at, and I can't blame anyone for that but myself."

Her father shook his head. "You are not and never have been a failure. When your mother and I speak, we are both in awe of how beautiful, strong, and smart you are. She sees it even if she doesn't say it. Get the divorce and live YOUR life. Stop worrying about anyone else because we made our choices. You saw what our decisions did to us, and you don't have to follow that road."

"Would you still marry her, even knowing what would come?" she asked cautiously.

"In a heartbeat. Your mother was my soulmate. We didn't have the right ingredients to carry it into forever," he confessed. "Besides, we made you. I'd do it all again to be able to sit here with you now. When it was good, it was magical. And you..." he hesitated. "Would you?"

She knew what he was asking. "The day we married, I wished someone would ask me if I was sure, but no one did. There were days we'd laugh until we cried, moments no one else would understand. I wouldn't be who I am today if it wasn't for that relationship." Tori thought about it for a moment. "Yes. I guess I would. I walked into it, not knowing anything about what I deserved. Before I left Craig, I saw the direction my mental health was going in and how the rest of my life would play out. I couldn't do it. I told him if it came down to him or me... it wasn't gonna be me. That little vision probably saved my life, Dad. I was so damaged."

He nodded. "If nothing else comes from this, I hope you never feel like you have to go through everything alone again. Aht...don't interrupt me. You're strong, and I'm proud of you, but you deserve better than what you got."

She hoped he was right. Tori pulled back from their embrace. "Thank you. Can we get to the movie before I start crying again?"

He laughed and grabbed the remote. They marathon-watched their favorite films until he had to leave. "Let me know when you make it home," Tori called out as she closed the door.

Chapter 25

WITSEC

Tori looked around; the apartment seemed so empty now that her father had gone. As much as she loved her Dad, she still felt anxiety whenever someone was in her space—a complete turnaround from before. Tori and Craig filled their house with people as often as possible, drinking away their seething rage toward each other. Did those same friends realize they were a buffer? Living blocks in the way of another argument, another fight, another—

Indignant meows from Hank and Shadow alerted her to their empty bowl. Tails erect, they circled her like furry sharks. Tori shook the bag of cat food, realizing it was almost empty. She did the math— ten dollars left to her name. She'd go to the store tomorrow. Hank gently nipped at her ankle to speed up the pour.

"Sorry, loves." Tori filled the bowl halfway. Hank looked up at her in annoyance. His soft growl translated to "To the top."

"Make it enough." She said. They stared at each other until Shadow flicked her with her tail. "I'll buy more tomorrow." Hank reluctantly bowed his head to eat.

Greedy ass cats.

Tori looked at the clock. "Midnight. I should go to bed."

Who was she kidding? Sleep wasn't going to come any time soon.

Tori weighed her options; clean the house or take a bath. She looked at the sink full of dishes, realizing she'd be angry with herself if she put the chores off until tomorrow.

As she washed the dishes, Tori replayed the conversation with her father. After all these years, he still considered Vivian his soulmate.

Tori wasn't sure if she was more disturbed by that prospect or the more destructive parallels in her marriage.

Unlike most of her friend's parents, whenever they weren't fighting, her mother and father seemed pulled toward each other like magnets. Her favorite bedtime story as a child was about their first date. She would clutch her bear at night, replaying the story of the day a woman who looked like his favorite actress walked into his life. As they told it, lightning struck the moment they locked eyes.

They got engaged in two weeks, married in 5 months, and a year later, she was born. Love at first sight, they called it. Maybe that was what she had been searching for. How many nights had she prayed to experience that same jolt? No matter how hard Tori tried to delude herself, Craig hadn't been that.

And a delusion it was. Her parents might have had love at one point, but they weren't happy. Happy marriages didn't leave children cowering under furniture.

"Get back," her father screamed, his heavy hand striking a blow across her chest, sending Tori down to the floor. The butcher knife Vivian had thrown was lodged in the wall in the space she had been standing milliseconds before. He stepped in front of her, pleading with Vivian to calm down and stop.

"GET OUT AND TAKE THAT DUMB BITCH WITH YOU!" her mother screamed, barely giving them time to grab shoes before a hail of ceramic plates began to fly in their direction.

Tori sat beside him in the car, shivering in thin pajamas and sneakers.

"Can we go somewhere?" she asked. Glancing anxiously at the house, afraid her mother would assault her again.

"No. She'll be angrier if we leave." He sighed. "Your mother will open the door in a few hours."

Some fairytale, she thought. In her experience, the carriage always turned out to be a pumpkin, and her dates always turned out to be rats. Who was she kidding? Fairytales were for suckers.

Not tonight, Tori. she chided herself, pushing away her intrusive thoughts as she focused on the task at hand.

Surprisingly, tidying up the mess didn't take long. Tori looked at the clock; 1 am—time for option number 2.

"Alexa, play music," Tori said as she stepped inside the tub. The scalding hot water made her hiss quietly as she got acclimated to the temperature. She laid back, tapping her fingers on the tub's edge to the beat. "Alexa, stop!" Tori called out. She sat in the water, watching leftover beads drip from the faucet, causing ripples on the surface.

Combined with the water's heat, the room's silence began to feel oppressive. Needing an outlet for her anger, Tori rolled, dunking her head underwater to muffle the sound of her scream. *One...two... three...*she counted until she couldn't hold her breath any longer. Tori rolled onto her back, gulping for oxygen before submerging again. She watched bubbles float to the surface as air released from her mouth.

Forty...forty-one...forty-two. She wondered if tears count if they fall underwater.

Her heartbeat thundered in her ears, a comfort. Isn't it funny how fragile a heart is? Too long under this water, and it would stop. But suicide doesn't get you into heaven. Even Craig decried that ending as he told her how he would destroy her reputation without sacrificing his, "You're not gonna make me look like some Tyler Perry cliché."

You're lucky I don't look good in orange, she thought but bit her tongue. Instead, she laughed. "I resent that. I look better in a dress."

She used to drive over a bridge daily to get home while still with Craig. One day someone switched lanes without signaling. Tori veered into the right lane to avoid an accident. For a quick moment, she thought about driving over the edge and crashing into the water below.

If I died, then I wouldn't have to go home.

What would Craig do? Play the crying widower, pretending he didn't know why it happened until it was safe to move a mistress in. He'd probably be angry she managed to get past his reach and happy his secrets would die with her. Would the headlines read "secretly battered desperate housewife dies in car crash"? But if it ended on that bridge, all the shit-swallowing she'd done over the years would be worthless.

Tori wanted to live more than ever now. As Aaliyah told her patients, "If your heart is beating, you have a chance."

Fifty-eight, fifty-nine, sixty.

Tori lifted her head from the water, her body readjusting to the air. Hank padded into the bathroom and jumped on the tub's edge, watching her with amusement in his intelligent golden eyes.

"You look at me like I get on your nerves," she murmured, rubbing him with a wet hand behind the ears. The rumble of deep purring was his only response. She watched him contentedly. Maybe this was peace.

She had a packed schedule this week. She was in charge of the company karaoke party on Wednesday, had arbitration scheduled for Thursday, and Leslie wanted her to help decorate for her going away party on Saturday night. If the past few months were any indication, Tori's chances of wild adventures would go down astronomically with Leslie out of town. She had a lot of decisions to make. She wanted to take the job but would play it cool until she had an offer letter.

"Serious question, is our life better now than before?" she asked Hank as he stretched a reassuring paw toward her.

In a swift motion, Hank slapped his paw into the water, causing it to splash on her face. He sprinted away, leaving poor Tori sputtering.

"I take it that means to stop feeling sorry for myself and get out of the tub." With a sigh, Tori rose out of the water, taking extra care to massage shea butter into her skin.

The sound of keys jingling in the hallway startled Tori mid-rub.

"There's no boogeyman waiting, girl." She shook her head.

Tori crept to the front door, securing the chain just in case. Her building didn't have any security. She never thought she would get so attached to the place. When Tori first moved there, she chose the location for two reasons; it was the cheapest rent in the nicest building she could afford, and judging by the meth van parked down the street, no one would come looking for her. It didn't fit the bourgeois housewife image she had built with Craig.

Tori jokingly dubbed it her witness protection apartment but the moniker fit. That first couple of months had been hard. Tori jumped at every noise and shadow, unable to shake the oily sensation of being watched. One day, Tori got home at 2 am from an unexpectedly long day at work only to find her apartment door wide open.

Frightened, Tori dug in her purse, pulling out the illegal taser she swore she'd never need. "You're on your own now. If you won't get a gun, be ready to zap the fuck out of someone." Aaliyah had said when she'd given it to her.

Hands shaking, Tori did her best Samuel L. Jackson impersonation. "I'M ARMED AND DANGEROUS, MOTHERFUCKER!" she cried as she turned the lights on.

Tori searched each room, but nothing was out of order outside her open apartment door. The only strange thing she noticed was the cats were huddled together under her bed, seemingly too terrified to come out. She hadn't seen them do that since her last explosive fight with Craig.

When she told the police, they laughed. "Lady, you live on the first floor in a rough neighborhood; a crackhead would've stolen the paint off your walls given a chance. If the whole house wasn't empty, you probably forgot to lock the door."

Grating at their tone, she returned and rechecked the house, finding nothing amiss. Tori sat on the couch, feeling annoyed and foolish, when she noticed her mail wasn't in the right spot.

A creature of habit, Tori always left important mail on the table to go through when she had free time. She got up to investigate, realizing it was the $500,000 life insurance policy confirmation she had received a few days earlier.

Tori had felt oddly independent when she applied for the policy. There were so many small practical things she needed to think about now, like getting a new emergency contact. Naming Aaliyah, her primary beneficiary, was a no-brainer.

She was the only person Tori trusted to take care of anything that needed to be paid for and would make sure that her parents got their share. If she left it to her father, he'd probably blow it all on lottery tickets. If she left it to her mother...Well, Tori didn't want to go down that rabbit hole.

I must've moved it by accident, she thought, *filing it away in her drawer and going to bed.*

A knock on her door startled her two days later while cooking dinner.

"You've been served," a man said, handed her a plain manilla envelope, and hurried away.

Confused, she opened the envelope. It was an updated divorce demand from Craig. Tori scanned the documents, her blood running cold as she read his petition to the court, "Defendants must maintain life insurance with Plaintiff as sole, irrevocable beneficiary. "

Tori dropped the envelope as she slid to the floor. It was HIM. She hadn't even applied for the policy until months after leaving. She hadn't even updated her driver's license, just in case. How had he even found her?

Tori shook her head, snapping out of her memories.

"You're almost free," she whispered, returning to the bedroom. Seeking reassurance, Tori grabbed her bible from under the pillow but couldn't open it.

With a heavy sigh, she knelt. "I've had more misery than I think is my share, God. I've spent almost three decades trying to be obedient to my parents, to my teachers, to my husband…to you, and I'm fucking tired. My name isn't Job. Is this shit supposed to make me strong? For what? I've gone from one dangerous situation to another, and I still don't know what you want from me!"

This was wrong, and she knew it. Hadn't Sister Lenora spent years drilling it into her head that free will was a gift? It all boiled down to her own poor choices.

Tori's voice broke. "It's not that I don't have faith in you. I'm struggling to believe that you have a purpose for me. You've brought me through every situation I've ever had, but this one has cost me everything I thought I knew about who I am. Can you send me a sign? Just point me in the direction you want me to go, God, and I'll do it cause the only thing I'm sure of is something has to change."

"And I'm sorry about the cursing." She cringed. "You know my heart."

Tori ended her prayer and stood up to get back into bed, but the shea butter she had put on earlier had left the floor greasy. Her foot slipped, and Tori slid across the room before smacking face-first into the wall.

As she lay on the floor looking at the ceiling, Tori laughed hysterically. "Jesus, I was just trying to pray to you, not meet you yet."

Jumping off the bed, Hank sniffed her head and licked her face like a dog.

"This only happens to me." She groaned. The phone rang, forcing her out of self-pity.

Chapter 26

The Road Not Taken

Tori scrambled to answer it, carefully avoiding the oil streaks on the floor.

"Hey boo! I knew you'd be up. Whatcha doin'?" Aaliyah asked as her face filled the screen. The steady beeping of a heart monitor in the background signaled that she was at work.

"I almost met Jesus." Tori leaned over, grabbing a towel to cover herself.

"Did you take one of Paris's edibles again?" Aaliyah asked. "Last time you went on a rant about vibrators being a gift from God––"

Tori cringed. "Don't remind me. This time I bust my ass picking a fight with God over my poor life decisions."

"Bitch…what?" Aaliyah shook her head. "Only you."

"Don't laugh." Shaking her head, Tori looked over at Hank, who was happily engaged in licking a streak of shea butter off the floor. "Even the cats have issues. You think my shitty luck is contagious?"

"Nah, that was God's way of slapping you upside down." Aaliyah paused. "Are you nervous about this week? Everything is going to be OK."

"I'm pretending to be." Tori sighed. "I shouted at Dad during movie night."

"Damn, what'd he do?" Aaliyah asked.

Bitterness seeped into Tori's voice. "He told me my mother loves me."

"Ouch." Aaliyah sighed. "It's true, though."

"Not you too!" Tori groaned. "She doesn't even like——"

"I'm not her favorite person, but you've got to remember their whole generation was fucked up. My parents don't know how to communicate properly either," Aaliyah explained. "They thought they were making us tough with ass whoopings and screaming 'cause that's what they were used to."

"That would be easier to swallow if my mother treated other people that way. She's amazing to everyone but my dad and me. It's fucked up." Tori shook her head. "It's deeper than that. I listened to my father speak about what he went through and realized that part of me had looked down on him for not being abusive back— like maybe he hadn't loved her enough because he didn't put his hands on her. My views on love were fucked up."

"I know, sweetie." Aaliyah sighed. "But you didn't know any better. Now you do. As for your mother…. well, one day, she'll get past whatever baggage she's got, but that is not your burden to carry. You can't heal her by tearing yourself apart."

"My rational brain knows that you are right." Tori begrudgingly agreed. "She loves me, but it's the way Frankenstein loved his monster; she is proud of her creation and eager to destroy it simultaneously. Enough emotion, how's work?"

"Same shit, different bedpan." Aaliyah snorted. "I need you to update my resume. I'm sick of this place."

"What happened now?" Tori braced herself for another heart-wrenching story from Aaliyah.

"The hospital is two seconds from getting shut down. They keep cutting our hours, but I've got a connection at one a few miles away who can put in a good word for me. The new job would mean more money and fewer hours. I need SOMEBODY to work her magic." Aaliyah grinned, fluttering her long lash extensions at Tori.

Tori laughed. "Save it, Izma. I've got you." She'd played the part of Aaliyah's boss more times than Tori could count. "I'll tell them you're the best thing since sliced bread when they call."

"What about your job? Diane still on the warpath?" Aaliyah asked.

"Yep. I don't know how long I'll last without cursing her ass out." Tori fumed. "I swear she touched my hair while I was sitting at my desk, but when I turned around, she pretended nothing had happened."

"That bitch is lucky she didn't meet you when we were in high school. So young, so angry. You'd have broken her fingers." Aaliyah grinned. "If you decide to give in to the dark side, worst-case scenario, you've got another job. You just got this other offer."

Tori nodded. " I don't know how serious it is."

"You've got to stop waiting for the shoe to drop, boo. Did Paris's friend send you the paperwork?" Aaliyah admonished her.

Tori sighed. "Not yet. I can't shake the feeling that there's something terrible on the way, but then I ask myself, why would God give me these opportunities if I can't take advantage of them?"

"This is religion class all over again. Baby, the bad's gonna come regardless. That's just life." Aaliyah reminded her. "Healing takes time. Stop trying to rush through this like a to-do list."

"Your optimism is incredibly frustrating." Tori groaned

Aaliyah grinned. "It's one of my better qualities."

"Be a friend. Give me some new advice?" Tori sighed dramatically. "I'm tired of trying to figure this out alone."

Aaliyah rolled her eyes. "I AM your friend. That's why I'm telling you that you've got this. Sometimes you have to be OK with letting things play out. It's not a sign of failure to choose your peace. I know you're the strongest person, but you keep letting these people shake your confidence."

"That's not it. It's just this fear of making the wrong decision." Tori protested.

Aaliyah wasn't having it. "Sis, I love you, but you're so scared about making the wrong decision that you're too scared to admit what you want. Choose YOUR happiness. You've been trying to hold yourself to these impossible fucking standards for as long as I've known you. Stop trying to people-please everyone."

Tori sighed. "But--"

"No, Tori." Aaliyah stopped her. "When you decided to leave Craig, all you had was hope. And look at you now. Yeah, it's been tough, but you've figured it out. Don't backslide tryna worry about people who don't give a fuck about you in the long run."

"Damn, bitch. Loud much?" Tori had nothing better to say; arguing with Aaliyah would waste time.

Aaliyah rolled her eyes. "Let's not pretend you don't talk to me the same way when I'm throwing myself a pity party. Tori, stop trying to be a martyr."

Tori grinned. "So what you're saying is, self-sacrifice isn't a sign of worth?"

"Not unless you're Jesus. Walked on water lately?" She made the sign of the cross and waggled her eyebrows at Tori.

Tori smiled. "I hate you a little when you're right."

"Bullshit. I'm the best thing since sliced bread, remember? Do me a favor, stay out of the tub, go to bed, and stop borrowing tomorrow's problems for today." Aaliyah blew her a kiss before ending the call.

Tori looked at the phone in her hand and shook her head. Aaliyah had a skill for cutting through the bullshit Tori repeated in her head that no one else had matched.

I've got to carve out some time to update her resume tomorrow, Tori thought. As a single mom who worked 80-hour weeks as a nurse to support her family while attending school online, Aaliyah was pretty inspirational. Tori's mind was boggled that her best friend still found the energy to work, come home, cook, play, teach, and kiss boo-boos for her son, David.

At five years old, David was one of the highlights of her life. When he was born, Aaliyah asked Tori to be his godmother. Still shocked that they were at the age where they could be parents, neither of them had known at the time what a gift he would be. Tori loved listening to David teach her about his favorite animals for hours, and just like his mama, he was quick to call her out if he thought she wasn't paying attention.

The kid was brilliant, funny, and energetic; it would be a lie if she didn't look at him and sometimes got sad. It didn't happen often. She did her best to stamp out those thoughts as soon as they floated to the surface of her mind, but occasionally Tori wondered what life would've been like with one of her own. Maybe she could've been a good mom if the circumstances had been different.

She wasn't weird about it, though. After she left Craig, Tori decided to be the cool single auntie wasn't so bad, and if God wanted it to happen, he'd send the stork.

An involuntary loud yawn reminded Tori that she had to be up for work in 3 hours. Turning off the light, she lay down.

Tori rolled over, grunting in pain, the muscle spasm in her back and rolling bouts of nausea exacerbated by the leaky air mattress she lay on.

Shadow gave her a concerned look as she watched Tori from a safe distance. The poor cat had learned the hard way that an air mattress and sharp claws were a bad combination.

"You're not in pain. You can breathe through it." Tori murmured in between gasps. Except for the hum of the air conditioner, the house was silent. Thoughts of sneaking upstairs and bathing in the master bathroom to soothe the ache gave her hope. Do I have enough time? She wondered.

She looked at the clock; 3 pm, and Craig wasn't home yet. Another Sunday in the office, he'd claimed when she saw him earlier.

Keeping tabs on each other was just a formality at this point. "As long as we're not fighting," was her motto.

Tori nodded. "My back's killing me, so I'm not going anywhere." She doubted he heard her as he closed the door.

It had been two months since she started sleeping in the basement. Craig didn't like coming down there. She was glad. It was her one safe space in the house while she searched for an apartment. They stayed out of each other's way as much as possible.

A woosh of air escaped from the hole she couldn't find, causing her to sink a little lower into the plastic mattress. Thoughts of laying down in their beautiful double pillow top California king mattress upstairs entered her mind; Tori didn't want to risk it. She told him he could keep it when she moved out. There was no way she wanted to take it to her new place.

*Another wave of pain rocked her. **Fuck this**, she thought. Tori crawled up the stairs to the bathroom, where they kept their medicine. Leaning on the sink, she searched through the bottles until she found what she was looking for. She hated having to take painkillers, but enough was enough. She shook out two pills and cupped her hand under the faucet, trying to swallow enough to wash them down.*

"Please don't let me throw up, Lord." She prayed. Just 2 hours ago, Tori had been in the same spot throwing up what felt like everything she'd ever eaten. The tramadol had begun to kick in by the time she reached the bed. Thank God, she thought as sleep took over.

The sensation of being shaken pulled her out of her sleep. "You don't look so good. Let's get you upstairs where you'll be comfortable," she heard. Tori's eyelids felt heavy as she tried to focus on what Craig was saying.

She felt weightless as he carried her up the stairs, depositing her gently on the bed.

"Isn't this better?" Craig whispered as he stroked Tori's hair away from her sweaty face.

Deep in her painkiller-induced haze, "Mmhmm" was all she could say.

He placed a finger over her lips. "Relax. I've got you."

Tori sighed in relief. He's being kind to me; she registered with surprise.

Sleep called to her as she sank back into the comfort of the bed, absently registering the feel of him getting in as well.

"You still don't wear underwear," he chuckled.

A moment later, she felt echoes of sharp pain as Craig thrust into her. His heavy frame smothered her as he pressed his shoulder into her throat. Tori struggled weakly, trying to turn her head so that she could breathe while he pumped away at her body like she was a doll.

"Stop," she whispered into his chest, but he didn't seem to hear her. Tori's arms felt like rubber as she tried to push him away. Each time he heard her make a noise, he leaned heavily on her throat, a warning to let him finish.

"This is all you needed. I'm going to knock you up tonight," he panted over her.

The pain of realizing what was happening transcended her disgust at his words. If I lie still, maybe he'll stop, she thought.

"You're not leaving me. I own you," Craig growled, trying to mark his territory.

Tori retreated into her mind, drowning out his words while she counted. One...two...three...

Tori's future played across the ceiling like a movie only she could see. It would be so easy just to let it happen.

Timed with his thrusts, she saw the houses, cars, and kids, arrogant brats who looked just like him, who despised her for being weak. Tori saw the depression she'd sink into and the razors she'd contemplate drawing across her skin. The number of pill bottles in her cabinet would make Jacqueline Suzanne blush. She'd have dolls for every occasion; white polygons for anxiety, red ovals for the STI she'd get after his next liaison with a secretary, and more of the tramadol, so she only felt hints of the force he used against her. Tori saw the lifetime of misery she'd have until she finally chased that sunset over the side of the bridge.

The images made her sick, bringing Tori back into her body. No, she thought.

She tried her arms again, still weak. Tears filled her eyes. "God, if you can hear me. Make him stop," she prayed under her breath.

A moment later, God answered her prayer when his phone rang. Craig rolled off of her and answered, "Hey, Sis." His tone as he walked away was more cheerful than she'd heard in months.

Tori lay there dazed as she watched him walk out of the room. She got up on unsteady legs and hurried into the master bathroom. Barely making it to the toilet, the vomit Tori had held back spewed out of her into the toilet.

Leaning over, she turned the water on for a shower and stepped in. Tori mechanically washed, scrubbing her skin until she noticed a pink tinge to the water swirling down the drain. "He'll never get to touch me again," she promised herself.

A hard knock alerted her to his presence. "Get dressed," he shouted through the door. "My sister and her boyfriend are coming over. They'll be here in an hour."

Like always, the loud screech of her alarm clock jolted her out of the dream. Groaning, she turned it off and got ready for the day.

Chapter 27

Hard-ER

B etween party prep and last-minute calls with Frank, Monday and Tuesday passed like a blur.

Errol was out of town again, and unsurprisingly, Diane had dropped all the party-planning responsibilities in her lap.

Since they had given her a generous budget and instructions to center it around a karaoke theme, Tori wasn't complaining much. By the time she was done, the office was almost unrecognizable.

The freelance decorators she hired had done a great job setting up a stage in the lobby with full performance lights. Tori checked in with the bartenders and chef (some weird associate of Diane's that she insisted was the best) to ensure they were fully stocked while the DJ finished checking the amps. This would be a party to remember if everything went according to plan.

"Where are you?" she messaged Paris. He hadn't shown up for work today. She was a little worried. It was unlike him to leave her on read.

Tori put her phone away, focusing instead on the first person brave enough to get on the microphone. She walked to the bar, ordering a vodka soda.

"Tori! You did such a great job," Lana interrupted with a smile. "Are you going to sing?"

"Probably not. Besides, I don't think anyone can top this." Tori nodded toward the stage where Eugene from accounting struggled through a song she didn't recognize.

Lana grimaced. "A dying animal would sound better."

They were too distracted by his ear-splitting attempt to hit a high note to notice Diane and her crew approach.

"Have you picked your song yet?" she asked Tori, ignoring Lana's presence.

Diane's sweet saccharine voice didn't match the vicious expression on her face.

Poor Lana melted behind her, using Tori as a human shield to cover her exit.

"No," she answered politely. "I'm happy to cheer everyone on from the audience."

Diane smiled. "Good. We will do a group song later. Make sure you've got your camera out." She walked away with everyone but Alan trailing behind her.

After a few steps, she realized he wasn't there. "Are you coming?" Diane asked, clearly annoyed.

Alan nodded. "I'll be right there. I'm getting a drink."

Diane walked away with her nose lifted in the air.

"I really hate that bitch," said Alan, his eyes following her as Diane walked away.

Eyes wide, Tori chortled. "That was not what I was expecting you to say."

"I'll have what she's having," he told the bartender, nodding toward Tori's drink.

"Blame it on the alcohol, Tori," Alan grunted as he swallowed his drink whole. "She plays a lot of games. I can't figure out why you're still here."

Tori gave him the side eye. "What do you mean?"

He stirred his drink with a straw. "You're better than this place. We all know how she treats you."

"Should you be talking about your friend like this?" Tori asked suspiciously.

"Friends? Hardly." He scoffed. "Diane promised me a promotion, but she decided to give it to someone else."

She winced. "I heard about that."

"Yeah, well, you be careful with her." A calculating look crossed Alan's face as he watched Diane hug Roger from across the room. "She doesn't have anything good planned for you."

Tori tilted her head. "What does that mean?"

"Just take my word for it," Alan said as he tossed back another drink and walked away.

"What the hell was that?" Tori wondered, sick of these games.

Her phone beeped; a message from Jonathan. "Hey. Check your email. I sent over the updated offer letter. Give it a look, and let's talk about your start date after you sign."

Hands shaking, Tori glanced around the room. Nobody would notice if she disappeared for a couple of minutes. She slipped away from the party, walked to her cubicle, and quickly read through the offer.

"150K, unlimited vacation, equity after a year, flexible hours, a company matched 401(k), and full healthcare." She wanted to cry.

Just then, a heavy thump followed by muffled laughter reached her. Somebody was in the copy room. Thinking someone was probably stealing office supplies while everyone was distracted, Tori walked in to warn them.

"Oh, shit!" She squealed, unprepared for the sight in front of her. Tori pulled the door closed and scurried to the bathroom. Pushing the stall doors open to make sure no one was hiding in there, Tori let out a loud hoot, "What the fuck!"

The sight of Alan's pale pimpled ass with Roger's legs wrapped around him like an erotic wheelbarrow was permanently burned into her brain. Roger's expression of ecstasy turned into horror as they locked eyes over Alan's shoulder in the split second before she hurried out.

If only he hadn't seen her.

"Why did it have to be me?" Tori groaned, leaning her head against the mirror. Could she go back to the party? No. She didn't want to stick around for whatever was coming next.

Tori exited the bathroom, hoping to grab her purse and leave, only to run into the pair coming from the copy room.

"Wait!" Roger called, but she was too focused on getting away to stop.

Tori broke into the most dignified half-sprint she could manage, grabbed her purse, and headed to the lobby.

"There you are!" Diane's voice was the last thing she wanted to hear. "Just in time; I'm going up now."

Tori gritted her teeth as she stopped. A rap song started playing as Diane, and her cronies got on the stage. Tori was so busy thinking about the scene she interrupted between Alan and Roger that it took a moment to register what was happening. Diane had chosen a song with a ton of N-words and was not censoring herself.

Tori took a few steps forward, trying to figure out what she would do.

The song finished a moment later, and Diane got off the stage to scattered applause.

She walked over to Tori with a wicked smile on her face. "How did we do?"

"Have you lost your damn mind?" Tori asked. "How dare you walk over and ask me if I liked it? That was disrespectful and ignorant."

Diane scoffed. "It's not like I called you a Nigger."

Audible gasps rippled across the room.

All the anger she'd held back rose to the surface, but Lana grabbed her by the arm before she could act.

"Don't do this," she whispered into Tori's ear.

Tori had had enough. Breathing hard, Tori grabbed her purse and looked Diane in the eye. "I might've been less offended if you were talented, but the only thing you'll ever manage to be is a disgusting, miserable human being."

She looked around the room at her (former) coworkers and walked out.

Tori felt like she was in a daze until she made it home, losing a spirited internal argument about what she should've/could've done until she finally heard back from Paris.

"I wanted to punch that bitch in the face," she said when he FaceTimed her. "Last time something like this happened, I was with Craig at one of his conventions. We had to let a white couple know they were one more "nigga" away from getting their ass beat. But I can't keep fighting my way out of every situation."

Paris laughed. "Girl, I'm so proud you didn't. I'm sorry that I couldn't be there today."

"So you could watch me get myself fired?" Tori groaned. "Why didn't you come?"

Paris sighed. "Well, there is no better way to say this. I'm leaving."

Tori was lost. "Leaving? To go where?"

"I'm moving to Italy. Marco got offered a job out there, and he has to leave by the end of the month," he told her.

Tori's jaw dropped. "I don't understand. That's less than two weeks."

"I know, but…I can't lose him." The pain in Paris's voice was palpable.

Tori laughed. "Oh honey, you won't lose him."

"I almost did." Paris's sad expression made Tori pause.

"What aren't you telling me?" she asked.

Paris sighed. "Marco— he wants to take a break."

Tori hesitated. "But why would he ask you to go with him if that's the case?"

"He didn't, but I'm going to convince him," Paris declared. "Before you say anything else, I know what this sounds like. I'm grown, and I know what I want."

Tori sighed. "Paris, I'm not going to tell you how to live your life, but are you sure this is what you want?"

He shrugged. "No, but I'm sure I want to spend the rest of my life with this man."

"I'm going to miss you like crazy." She smiled sadly, "Well, ain't this some shit. I'm unemployed, and you're going on an overseas adventure. Just send my key to your new place in the mail."

"You are not unemployed. Stop waiting and sign that letter!" he reminded her. "You'll be happier working with Jonathan than you've ever been with Errol."

Tori nodded. "You're right. Between that witch and the mess with Roger, my mind hasn't even processed what happened."

"What does Roger have to do with this?" Paris asked.

Tori bit her lip. "Uh, you have to promise me not to say anything...to anyone...ever!"

"Cross my heart," he swore.

Tori cringed. "Before Diane pulled her bullshit, I caught him in a very compromising position."

"With who? What did you see?" Paris asked gleefully.

She hesitated. Somehow telling Roger's secrets didn't seem right. "More of him than I'd ever want to see."

"You're not going to tell me, are you?" he sighed. "I'll let it go for now, but you don't owe that man any loyalty."

"I know. Let's focus on you and your plans," she deflected.

He nodded, "I'm going to hold off on the proposal until we get settled over there. I'm not going to let this be an obstacle for us. "

Tori listened to Paris talk about his plans for his new home, saying a silent prayer that things would work out. He didn't want to hear what she had to say; Paris just wanted someone to be happy for him.

For everything he had done for her, that was the very least she could do.

When Tori finally went to bed, her unspent anger with Diane, sadness at Paris's news, and anticipation over sitting face-to-face with Craig had depleted her energy. She couldn't afford to feel drained like this anymore.

"God, I just want to be free of everything holding me back or standing in the way of my happiness." She prayed, and for the first time in a long time, Tori didn't dream at all.

Chapter 28

Yellow Brick Rainbow

Tori's father covered her with an umbrella as they approached the attorney's office. "Are you gonna be OK in there?"

Tori smoothed her dress with her free hand, "Yes." Realizing how small her voice sounded, she cleared her throat. "It will all be over soon."

Frank greeted them by the front door, ushering them quickly into an empty office on the right. Across the hall, she caught a glimpse of Craig seated at a conference table with his attorney and the mediator before Frank closed the door.

"So, are you prepared for the conversation today?" Frank asked as he shuffled the papers on his desk.

Tori was distracted, her mind running through the details she'd seen.

Something wasn't right. Craig was wearing a suit that she had bought him before she left. He looked thin. His skin was sallow with inflamed razor bumps, and judging from the glare on his head, his hair was almost gone. At what point did that happen? Something in her heart went out to him.

"Yes," she said absently, still thinking about how pitiful he looked.

"Great." Frank smiled. "So I've written up a list of your non-negotiables––"

"Frank…" she interrupted, "…I want to be divorced today."

Frank smiled. "We just have to go in and talk about the final figure if you agree to it today."

"I will waive all my rights to the business we started. Craig can have everything in the house and the cars." Tori paused. "I want him to pay the leftover medical bills and your fees."

Frank looked like he had been struck by lightning, "…but that only comes out to about 10K? You can get way more than that."

"Tell him it's a one-time offer, and if he doesn't accept in the next five minutes, that it's off the table, we will go through with the mediation." Tori's tone brooked no argument.

"Tori, are you sure?" her father asked, sharing a look with Frank.

"Yes," she squeezed his hand.

Turning to Frank, she nodded. "Make the offer."

Frank shook his head as he walked out of the room.

"Tori, I don't understand." Her dad shook his head. "I thought you wanted to confront him."

"So did I." She sighed. "I think I was angry until now, but now...I want this over with."

Tori took a deep breath. "I already did the worst thing I could've done to him. I left. He never believed I'd do it. I saw him for a second as we came in. He looks sick. He'll have to spend the rest of his life manipulating people to get ahead. I don't want to rot from the inside the way he is. The best thing I can do now is to move on with my life and leave him to his demons."

Frank opened the door. "Good news, he agreed. I can draft the documents and send everything to you today."

"Are you serious?" Tori asked, waiting for a catch.

"It's done. Once you both sign, I'll file it with the court, and he can't renege." Frank shook his head. "This is the best offer he's ever going to get. You gave him a victory."

"Not from where I'm sitting. I appreciate your help with this, Frank. Now that this is over, I'll call you later. I need your advice on another matter." Tori smiled, shook his hand, and left the office with her father trailing behind her. From the corner of her eye, she saw Craig step out of the conference room to intercept her.

With her head held high, she walked past him and out the door. The rain had stopped, and a beautiful ray of sunshine warmed her as she walked to the car.

Tori sent a group message to Paris and Aaliyah. "I did it. I got my freedom back."

As the congratulations rolled in, she saw an email notification from Lana requesting she meet with Diane and the legal team the next day.

She chuckled and read the message to her father, "I guess they decided to fire me. I have to go to the office and pick up my stuff anyway."

"Might as well get rid of all the baggage at once." he laughed. "Victoria Rose, I'm proud of you. You're officially divorced and already got a new job. Walk in there tomorrow and tell them to kiss your Black ass."

She laughed. "Thanks, Dad. I'm positive I did the right thing."

"Wow. Look at that," he said, pointing in front of them.

Tori looked up from the phone to see what he was talking about. On the other side of the window was a bright rainbow. She quickly pulled out her camera to take a picture of the sky when she noticed where they were. It was the same bridge she had thought of ending her life on a few years before.

"Thank you, God," she whispered as they crossed the end, watching it pass in the rearview mirror.

She laughed at the irony.

Her dad looked over in confusion, "What's funny?"

"Everything." She shook her head. "It all worked out the way it was supposed to."

Tori promised her dad she would call him the next day with updates after he dropped her off.

She kissed the cats until they squirmed and walked around her empty apartment, trying to figure out what to do on her first night as a legally single adult in a decade.

Grabbing a bottle of wine from the fridge, she settled on masturbation and a celebratory hangover. Delicious.

When the alarm clock went off in the morning, Tori ignored it; there was no purpose in rushing to get fired. Her meeting wasn't until 11. She figured they picked a time with the least people there to witness.

Paris texted that Diane and her husband had spent half an hour arguing in the conference room, and everyone was waiting for part two of the showdown, "Hurry up and get here so I can resign right after your meeting."

She felt different for some reason and took extra care in picking out her outfit, throwing on a pair of Louboutins and a badass Dundas sheath dress that she hadn't given away from her former life. In her mother's words, "You can't go into a battle unarmed or underdressed."

When she got to the office, Tori felt like she was going to an old cowboy showdown. Her former coworkers scattered like tumbleweeds as she walked into the building.

She walked straight to her cubicle and turned on the computer, quickly wiping it of any leftover personal files.

The sound of a throat being cleared made her pause. "Tori, can I talk to you?" Roger asked nervously.

She didn't bother turning around. "I have a meeting with your wife in a few moments."

He shuffled his feet nervously. "I know, but this will just take a second."

Tori followed him into an empty office, keeping her hand on the doorknob.

"Listen about the other day…."

She raised a hand to stop him. "That is not my business."

Roger nodded. "Thank you for saying that, but you know what you saw—"

"Is not my business. You are an adult." Tori turned the doorknob to leave.

"I want to help you…." he blurted out, "…I know you and my wife have not had the best relationship."

She held back a snort but couldn't control her eyebrow twitch.

"I know that you contribute a lot to this company, and maybe there's something that we could do to help each other." He searched her face for signs of hope. He seemed to be searching for the right words.

Is this motherfucker trying to bribe me? she wondered.

"What do you mean?" she asked. "I'm unsure what you're referring to, but what would help me would be a letter of recommendation for my next position."

"Oh, that's not a problem; what else?" he asked.

"This is not bribery, Roger. I've worked very hard for this company and spent years investing in what you're doing for the future. I would like for my next role to be sent off respectfully."

"Are you sure you don't want to stay?" he asked, surprised.

Diane entered the room with an attitude. "You were supposed to meet us in the conference room."

Tori maintained her composure. "Your husband asked to speak to me."

"Let's not drag this out," she said, leaving the door open so everyone in the office could hear, a humiliation tactic that wasn't lost on Tori.

She followed Diane into the conference room, where Harry from the legal department was waiting.

"Victoria..." he shook her hand, "...let's have a seat. Before we begin...."

Diane huffed. "You are being terminated for inappropriate behavior at our company party."

My God, this bitch is delusional, Tori thought.

Across the table, she made eye contact with Roger, who turned beet red from embarrassment.

"Diane--" Roger and Harry interjected, hoping to keep her from saying anything else.

Harry cleared his throat. "We are prepared to offer you a generous severance package to avoid further unpleasantness." He slid a folder across the table to her.

Tori scanned it, closed the file, and sat back, stroking the arm of the chair. "You're offering me two weeks of severance?"

"Yes, contingent upon you signing an NDA," Harry added, looking uncomfortable.

"I see." Tori slid the folder back across the table. "Unfortunately, I cannot sign this. After being publicly humiliated, harassed, and verbally accosted with racial slurs, not to mention the well-documented aggressive treatment that I've received from members of this company, and that per Diane's instructions, the most recent incident was recorded, I've conferred with my attorney. We are prepared to fight my wrongful termination in court."

Diane's smug face turned ashen at every word from Tori's lips. For once, she had nothing to say.

Roger nodded. "I think we can work something out."

When they finished talking, Diane had broken out in hives, and poor Harry was utterly bewildered. "Victoria, I'll have the updated agreement ready in five minutes," he said as he hurried to the printer.

Diane sneered as Harry left the room before turning her fury on Tori. "You think…"

Tori leaned closer to her. "I know it would be wise for you to walk away before you say something that makes me call Harry back to the table."

Harry came back in with the documents and a pen for Tori. She read the file, said an internal prayer, and signed.

The door opened. To everyone's surprise, Errol popped in. "Hello, all. What's happening here?"

Diane looked as though she saw a ghost. "Daddy! We're just finishing up."

Tori closed the folder and handed it back to Harry. "Yes. Today is my last day. Thank you for the opportunity to be a part of the company."

Errol was confused. "I don't understand. Are you sure you want to leave? I just talked to Diane about giving you a promotion. Maybe we can work something out."

The last of the color blanched from Diane's face to Tori's amusement.

She raised an eyebrow. "I was under the impression you were planning to sell soon?"

"How did you––" Errol cleared his throat. "No…our buyer pulled out recently."

Interesting, she thought, storing that away for future consideration.

Tori smiled. "Thank you for the offer. Perhaps we can discuss something on a consulting basis in the future. I'll email you my direct contact information."

She shook Errol's hand and exited the conference room just in time to see Paris walk over with a sheet of paper in his hand.

"Is that what I think it is?" she whispered when he was close.

Paris winked. "Mhmm, I'm going to drop it on the table now. Drinks around the corner in 5?"

"I'll be at our table." Tori walked away to say goodbye to the few staff members she liked, hugging Lana and wishing her good luck.

As she walked out of the building for the last time, she ran into Alan.

They didn't exchange a word, but his sly smile spoke volumes as Alan glanced between her and a harried-looking Diane, who seemed to be getting an earful from her father.

Tori winked, walking out of the building with a spring in her step that had been missing for a long time.

As she walked toward the restaurant, her phone rang. Surprised, she answered, "Hey, Marco."

Chapter 29

Powder Puff Girl

"20 weeks of severance? How did you manage that?" Leslie asked as they decorated the table.

"They offered me two weeks without telling the lawyer what really happened at the party. Once I started listing details and refused to sign the NDA, they were willing to negotiate," Tori explained as she nibbled on a celery stalk.

Leslie laughed. "Well, what will you do next?"

Tori shook her head. "I haven't figured that out yet. I signed the offer letter for the new job, and I don't have to start for a few weeks. I only know that as soon as the check clears, I'm signing up for teletherapy."

Leslie laughed. "Everyone should be here soon," she said, putting the final touches on the table. "Think they'll like it?"

"Everything looks great. Thanks for letting Paris combine his going away party with yours." Tori stepped back and surveyed their work. "What time does your flight leave tomorrow? Are you excited to visit your family?"

"Somewhat. It may take me longer than I thought to get back. I'm having a minor visa issue." Leslie sighed.

Tori was surprised. "Still? I thought you figured everything out."

"I haven't booked anything in a while, so the agency won't sponsor me." Leslie sat down on one of the barstools twiddling her thumbs.

Tori frowned. "I know you said it won't work, but how about you ask your father again to hire you? Didn't you tell me he was having issues with his staff here?"

Leslie nodded. "Yes, but he'll say no."

"Ask him to give you a job that allows you to keep an eye on things, and you can report back to him. Something helpful enough that he might consider it," Tori suggested.

Leslie nodded. "That's better than what I thought."

"What were you thinking?" Tori asked.

"Well..." Leslie cleared her throat, "...I figured we could get married."

Tori wrinkled her nose. "We who?"

"You and I." Leslie smiled at her as though it was a viable option.

Tori fell out laughing. "Teeny little problem, no one would believe we are together. The ink isn't even dry on my divorce papers."

Leslie nodded. "I thought about that too. I can fill out the papers now, and once you get the final decree, come back on the fiancée visa."

Tori stopped laughing. "You're serious?"

Leslie walked over to her dresser and pulled out a ring box. Turning to Tori, she got down on one knee.

"Will you marry me so I can stay in the country?" Leslie grinned.

Tori froze, looking from the ring to her friend in a panic. "Uh…this wasn't on my bingo card."

"Think about it," Leslie said, slipping the ring on her finger. "We're best friends. I love you. You love me. You already have a key to the house. Just move in."

Tori shook her head. "Uh, you must want my mother to actually kill me. Besides, I like my apartment."

Leslie rolled her eyes."OK. We'll tell her the truth. It's not like we're sleeping together. I can stay in the country, and we can divorce in a couple of years." Leslie said reasonably. " Besides, I need you. Who else is going to keep me out of trouble?"

The doorbell rang, announcing the first guests. Tori stood there, shell-shocked, as Leslie ran to the door. "Hiiii! Thank you for coming. Just throw your stuff in the guest room."

Tori studied the ring on her finger, a princess cut surrounded by two smaller diamonds on its side, similar to the ring from Craig. She fought the urge to throw it across the room.

"You look like a deer in headlights." Paris's voice interrupted her thoughts.

Snapping a smile on her face, Tori hugged him. "I feel like one. When did you get here?" She looked around the room; it had filled up faster than she had realized.

He planted a big kiss on her cheek. "A few minutes ago. Hopefully, this party will be less eventful than the last. Are you OK? Still thinking about yesterday?"

She shook her head. "No. I-it doesn't matter. I still can't believe you're leaving so soon. Are you packed?"

"Ugh, not even a suitcase." He worried his lip. "I'm debating leaving everything behind. If I'm going to chase this man, I might as well go full movie romance."

"I doubt that's going to be necessary." She laughed. "Speaking of... where is Marco?"

Paris gestured toward the guest room. "He's putting our coats away."

"I'm gonna go say hi. Go grab a drink; I'll find you in a bit." Tori set off in search of Marco.

She found him standing in the middle of the guest bedroom, looking at a small box in his hand. He stuffed it into his pocket at her entrance. "Hey gorgeous, you gave me a heart attack!"

Tori gave him a big hug. "Sorry. I practically ran away from Paris. I'm so excited. Do you know what you're going to say?"

Marco nodded sheepishly. "I have something written down. Want to read it?"

Tori shook her head. "I'm sure it's beautiful. Just speak from your heart. That man loves you. He's going to cry his eyes out."

"I hope so." He grinned.

"Now..." she straightened his collar, "...gather your courage and sweep my friend off his Louboutins."

Tori gave him one last hug before they walked out of the room together.

Paris walked over with drinks for her and Marco. "Soooo, you weren't going to say anything?"

"Huh?" she asked; Marco's puzzled expression on her face matched hers.

Paris grabbed her hand. "Leslie said you're getting married so that she can stay."

Tori narrowed her eyes, scanning the room for her. "She did, did she?"

He nodded. "I noticed the ring before, but I thought you were wearing your old one as a morbid post-divorce fuck you."

"No. Leslie blindsided me right before everyone got here. I didn't say yes." Tori fumed.

Paris shook his head. "Don't do it. You did not go through all that bullshit to get caught in some 90-day fiancée drama."

"It's not going to come to that." Tori laughed. "I'm surprised. I would've bet you'd say I could do worse than marrying her for my second time around?"

"Take it from me; when you get married again, it needs to be for the right reasons." Paris cleared his throat. "Speaking of, Marco...there is something I need to tell you."

Marco snapped out of his daze. "No, I need to say something first."

He got down on one knee. "You are my heart. I've watched you overcome your fears, and allow me the pleasure of loving you. We've spent the past few years building our life together, not wanting to wake up from this dream, even in our hard times. After they offered me this job, I didn't want to take it because no part of me wanted to separate you from the other people you love. I thought I was putting you first by saying we should take a break. I should've known that no one tells you what to do. When you told me that there was no way you were staying here without me, I remembered a truth that I tried to ignore. We belong together. Paris Alexander Stewart, marry me, and let's continue this adventure for the rest of our lives."

There was no dry eye in the room by the end of the speech. Everyone held their breath, waiting for Paris to say yes.

Chest heaving, he stood over Marco, silent for a moment.

"Yes, you son-of-a-bitch!" he cried. "You stole my proposal moment." Paris pulled a ring box out of his pocket.

The crowd erupted in cheers and congratulations as the happy couple exchanged rings.

Tori scanned the room for Leslie but didn't see her. Noticing a tall man standing in the corner, her eyes grew wide; it was Leslie's father.

She walked over to greet him. "Mr. Dalton, Leslie didn't mention you were in town. It's nice to see you."

He smiled. "Yes. Leslie said she was having a get-together tonight. I figured I would surprise her. I'm in the states for a business meeting."

That gave Tori a brilliant idea, "Really?" she asked, "Leslie's going to be so disappointed that she's missing it. She only talks about wanting to learn more about running a company."

"My daughter?" he scoffed. "She normally can't wait to leave. Too dull for her, I expect."

Tori tried to keep her confusion from showing. Leslie always said he didn't support her dreams.

Tori winked. "You would be surprised. I told her she should apply for an internship with you. Get to know the company at every level."

He nodded. "That would make her mother and I very happy." This was a weird turn but an excellent opportunity to save her from a proposal she didn't want.

Tori beamed. "Let me go track her down for you."

Two birds, one stone, Tori thought. She hurried to Leslie's bedroom to tell her about her father's surprise appearance.

The bedroom was empty, but she heard muffled laughter from the master bathroom. She groaned, "Haven't I caught enough people having sex?"

"Hey! Whoever's in there. Knock it off!" Tori tried the doorknob, but it was locked.

"Use the other bathroom. This one is off-limits." She knocked on the door again.

A guy she didn't know opened the door. "Uh, sorry. We'll be out in a minute."

"Who are you, and what's on your face?" Tori asked in confusion. The guy looked like he had patted his face with an old-fashioned powder puff. There was white residue on his forehead, lip, and the tip of his nose.

Tori's jaw dropped. "Is that cocaine?"

His glazed-over eyes grew wide as he lifted his arms in an exaggerated shrug. "What cocaine?"

Giggles alerted Tori to someone else's presence. She pushed the door open, finding Leslie hiding behind him with a nervous expression. Tori was shocked.

"Get out!" Tori growled at him.

"Hey…what's the problem?" the guy asked. "There's more if you want in."

"If you don't get the fuck out now, I'm going to call the police." Tori snarled at him.

"Whoa, whoa! I'm gone." He grabbed a backpack off the toilet seat. "See you later, Les. Your friend is trippin'."

He hurried away, slamming the bedroom door behind him.

"This is my first time trying it," Leslie said, her jaw quivering as the drugs kicked in. She swept the remnants into a pile, hesitating to knock it down the drain.

Tori raised her hand. "Don't lie. Cocaine?! Are you out of your mind? Do you know what that shit can do to you?" Her eyes widened. "Your nose bleed at that party! This is what Renee was trying to tell me last time."

"Huh?" Leslie looked in the mirror. "Don't make a big deal out of this. It's just a party drug. It's my last night here."

Tori shook her head. "While you were in here blowing a hole in your fucking nose, you missed Paris and Marco proposing to each other."

"Shit! Tori, I'm sorry," Leslie apologized. "Just give me a minute, and I'll be right there."

Tori shook her head. "You're going to need more than a minute. Your father is here."

"Don't be ridiculous." Leslie shook her head.

"Yeah, and we had a great conversation about you. He's interested in giving you a job." Tori took the ring off and placed it on the sink. "Now, you don't need to use me. I'm done. Have a safe flight."

"Wait! Tori—" Leslie called at her friend's retreating back.

Tori grabbed her stuff and rejoined the party, only to find Marco and Paris already on their way out.

"Perfect timing! Want a ride?" Marco asked as he helped Paris put on his coat.

"Yeah, I need to get out of here." She saw Leslie's dad walk toward the bedroom. "I'll fill you in outside."

Chapter 30

Fringe Benefits

Tori lounged across her couch, talking to Aaliyah, "I'm on a roll. In the past four days, I've lost my job, divorced, signed a new contract, negotiated a bomb ass settlement, got proposed to by a cokehead, and cut off a friend. Capt'n Save-Em is officially retired!"

"You must've finally said the right prayer. " Aaliyah laughed. "I knew I didn't like that girl."

"Tell me about it. Realizing that some friendships are meant to be seasonal was a valuable lesson." Tori paused. "Aaand…I'm finally going to go on vacation."

"That's fantastic! You deserve it." She smiled. "Where are you going?"

Tori grinned. "The check cleared this morning. I'm not sure yet, but I've decided not to limit myself. I'll take a solo trip to clear my head first and then visit you in Miami for a few days. "

"Really?" Aaliyah was surprised. "David will love that. He misses you."

Tori nodded. "I know. We can all go to Disney or something...." The phone beeped. "Shit, it's my mother. I've been ducking her calls since before court."

"If you hide any longer, she's gonna show up at your door," her friend cautioned.

Tori shivered. "You're right. I'll hit you back later, and we'll figure out the details. Love you!"

She clicked over to the other line. "Hey, Mo--"

"Was your phone broken?" her mother asked, not bothering with pleasantries.

"No." Tori rolled her eyes, grateful her mother couldn't see her. "It's been a hectic couple of days, and I haven't had time to talk."

"I had to learn from your father that you walked away from your divorce settlement with nothing," her mother scolded her.

Tori sighed. "I didn't walk away empty-handed. He has to pay off my old medical bills and any fees I get from my attorney. If there is anything left, I'm thinking of taking a trip somewhere for a few days."

At that, her mother's tone brightened. "Good. Where are you taking me?"

Tori was confused. "Umm...I'm going to take my Godson to Disney-land."

"Are you serious? After all I've sacrificed for you, you'd rather do something nice for them? How could you be so stupid?" Vivian's anger seeped through the phone.

"Ma...I love you, but I'm tired of how you talk to me." Tori shook her head. "I'm not ungrateful. I've idolized you, even when you were dead wrong. I've tried hard to make you proud, but your actions tell me I'm not good enough. I'm afraid to tell you whenever something good happens to me because you'll tear me down. No wonder you call me a disappointment. You can't spend the rest of your life holding it over my head that you clothed and fed me. You're my mother. That was your job! I don't owe you, and you don't own me. I've seen you treat strangers and animals better than me."

"I didn't raise you to think you could talk to me like that, you disrespectful little bitch!" Her mother yelled. "You think anyone will care about you the way I do? You wouldn't have a fucking thing if it weren't for me. You walk around with your nose in the air like you're not a piece of shit, just like your father. He was only good for breakfast in the morning and a pair of school shoes. You'd better learn to obey my word. All your little friends laugh at you behind your back. You're a disgrace. "

Tori lost it. " OBEY? Who?! The woman who called me stupid, ugly, and worthless my whole life? Give me a break, Mom! I've followed what you told me, and guess what... I wound up just as miserable as you and my father. That wasn't a life; it was a prison."

"Who the fuck do you think you're talking to!? Do you think anything you've done would've happened without me? All of the fabulous opportunities I've put in your lap, and you want to be ungrateful? You're not talented. You aren't smart. You would be nothing if it weren't for me." Her mother screamed into the phone.

Vivian's words rang hollow this time. " I don't know what to say to make you hear me. Mom, what made you change? It wasn't always like this. Was it because you weren't happy with Dad? What did I do to make you hate me so much?" she asked earnestly, ready to hear the truth.

"Don't be fucking ridiculous," Vivian growled. "The only thing I've ever done for you is sacrifice. You act just like your father. You need to read your bible and learn your place! Do you want to listen to that whore, Aaliyah, instead of your mother?! Once you met her, you became an ungrateful bitch. That's why you're alone now. Nobody respects you. When you see I'm right, you'll come crawling back like the prodigal child."

"Do you know what gives me comfort?" Tori sighed, "This isn't about me. I love you, Mom, but every evil word you've ever said to me is how you feel about yourself, and I'm sorry that someone put that pain in you, but you can't keep passing it down like an inheritance! The abuse has to end sometime. I'm tired of dealing with resentment from you that I didn't earn!"

Tori hadn't realized her words' truth until she said them aloud. "Jesus! You are quick to blame everyone except yourself for how our relationship is. Whatever hurt you before I was born is not my fault. Whatever happened with Dad wasn't my fault. Stop treating me like

I've destroyed your life! And I'm just like my father? The bar is set so fucking low in this family that all he had to do to be the good parent was not punch me around. Do you know how messed up that is? How can you give the world the best parts of you but take out your anger on me? We both need therapy if we're going to be in each other's lives because I can't keep doing this."

Her mother yelled, "Therapy?! You'd better find Jesus, you disgusting, selfish demon! I—"

"Goodbye, mom." Tori cut her off, ending the call.

She sat there for a moment, replaying the hurtful words Vivian had thrown at her until Tori began to cry. She cried for all the negative things she had been taught to believe about herself and all the pain Tori could have avoided if she had realized sooner that the self-hate she'd harbored didn't belong to her. That voice adding fuel to her intrusive thoughts and impostor syndrome hadn't been hers— it belonged to Vivian.

Afterward, Tori felt like a weight had been lifted from her shoulders. She didn't need breathing exercises to get past her pain for once.

Wiping her eyes, Tori grabbed her laptop and began to search for flights to Miami when a flight deal alert crossed her screen. This had to be fake. The alert said there were first-class nonstop round-trip flights from New York to Spain for $200, leaving the day before her birthday. After some digging, Tori saw from Spain that she could fly to Italy and France for $200 more. She triple-checked the site, and the numbers were legit.

No way. This is the deal of a lifetime! "Should I do this?" she asked herself. Tori thought about all the times she missed opportunities because she was too afraid to take a chance. "Not anymore," she said aloud. Tori quickly entered her credit card information and printed the receipt.

She grabbed her phone and called her father, "So… you snitched on me, and Mom predictably…was Mom. Fair warning, I just said things I needed to get off my chest, blocked her number…and booked a two-week trip to Europe for $444.33."

"Sorry, I let the cat out of the bag. I thought you had already told her," Tori's father apologized.

Tori shrugged. "It is what it is. She's part of the reason I decided to sign the papers. I traded one abuser for another because some unhealed part of me wanted to believe she was right and that this was what I deserved. I thought I was choosing myself when I left Craig, but I hadn't. I've been biting my tongue all this time, and that shit is poisonous. Something has to change. Maybe this trip is what I need."

"Europe? Tori, are you running away from home again?" he asked hesitantly.

She laughed. "Not at all. I can't pray for my life to be cleared of the bullshit while actively staying around it. I'm tired of healing and hurting at the same time. There are no more excuses left to hold me back."

"So when are you leaving to "eat, pray, love" your way through Europe?" her father asked.

Tori smiled. "Next week. The flight leaves the day before my birthday. I'll be back a few days before I start my new job. Who knows, I might decide to visit Paris in Paris."

He laughed. "So soon? It sounds like you're on the right track for another adventure."

Tori chuckled. "I'm starting a new chapter. I've got to fill it with something."

THE END!

Afterword

Yay! You made it to the end of "The Other Night"! Thank you for spending precious time with my book. I hope that you enjoyed it!

30+ years ago, when I handed my parents my first book report, I knew I wanted to create one of my own. This is me keeping that promise to myself.

Some of my earliest memories are centered around literature. My mother taught me to read, encouraging me to expand my mind with the richness and joy that a good book can bring while introducing me to the theatrics, culture, and glamour of the late 80s/early 90s on the East Coast. My father would take me to Barnes & Noble or the Borders at World Trade Center, observing the time so I could browse the shelves at my leisure until he needed to get to work for his 3-11 shift at NJ Transit. I still remember the faces of the cashiers who would ring us up while I babbled to anyone who would listen about what I imagined would be on its pages one day.

It brings me endless joy that even though times and locations have changed, I still have that same excitement when I pick up a new book. I hope that you have experienced the same with this.

Can I tell you a secret?

    This is not the book I intended to create.

"The Other Night" took a week to write and a year to re-write. I was so unsure of what this story was conveying that for all of 2022, if anyone out of my immediate circle asked for details, I said, "It's about a kidnapping and a series of unfortunate events, but that title is already taken, so I don't know what to call it." I couldn't articulate that although I was committed to the task, I had no idea what I was doing. Patience has never been my strong suit because, according to my parents, I walked before I learned to crawl.

Oddly enough, the almost-trafficking portion of the book is based on an actual event. On a night out with friends, we wandered into the wrong bar, had our drinks spiked, and got separated. Luckily, a couple of good Samaritans intervened, and our adventure did not turn into tragedy. Eventually, the event turned into an anecdote that my friends spent more time laughing over than I did. At least until a pandemic forced me to sit down and process how that brush with danger changed my outlook on life.

Organically-news of people (some within my circle) sharing similar experiences began to reach me at an alarming rate. Many revealed that they buried their stories and never sought support for fear of judgment. How many of us can say that emotional dissonance in processing our trauma keeps us stuck? How many areas of our lives are shaped by this, allowing gaslighting friends/family members, toxic workplaces, and abusive relationships to overtake our self-confidence? These revelations broke my heart and infuriated me, leading to a very introspective look at my coping mechanisms. No one wants to be a member of the trauma club, but how do you heal if you won't face your issues head-on? If you stand up for yourself, how do you know when to choose peace over pain? Can you laugh despite it all?

In writing fiction, I realized that Tori needed to go through her journey toward an understanding of areas of her life that needed to be fixed past her awful nightclub experience. Because of this, the book's tone had to change as she moved forward. Some questioned my choices, advising that stories like this only have an audience if the plot shifts into a romance. I took that as a challenge because while I wanted Tori and her circle to be funny, the subjects discussed in the book were decidedly not. I didn't want to trivialize my character's experiences and people worldwide who have gone through similar, but I also didn't want to distress my readers. I learned very quickly that molding the story to make everyone happy while staying true to the words in my mind was an exercise in futility. As my beloved Paris would say," That people-pleasing shit is dead."

Seven re-writes later, when I considered throwing my laptop into the nearest dumpster if I found another spelling error, I prayed for a sign and, like my main character, had a miraculous case of divine intervention. My laptop froze, and I accidentally clicked publish while moving the mouse to get it to UN-freeze. Basically, God said, "If you don't, I'll do it for you." I look back on that moment with gratitude. Nothing I have experienced in life matches my joy at having done what I set out to do. God is great.

Thank you again for reading "The Other Night." It has been an honor bringing this book to life, and I am so excited to continue Tori's story (in all its future forms) for you all. Stay tuned!

With Love,

THE OTHER NIGHT

Ashley Taylor

About the Author

Ashley is a New Jersey native whose love of writing started when her parents gifted her The Hobbit in Pre-K. With her signature sense of humor, Ashley explores topics like identity, loss, divorce, anger, love, healing, and friendship in her book and has already begun writing the sequel.

You can connect with me on:
- https://www.dearashley.com
- https://twitter.com/writedearashley
- https://www.instagram.com/writedearashley
- https://www.instagram.com/ataylorpublishing